The ship's cont... ...tion, and agent Selena Ash realized that someone else knew she was not the idle playgirl she seemed. Whoever had sent her into uncharted space against her will must have known of her mission to trace the path of a long-dead Space Scout and find a miraculous tree. But they could not have known that in her attempt to escape she would stumble upon the fabulous planet they sought.

It was a world like Paradise, perfect in its serenity, until the advent of man aroused its sleeping powers, forces which knew nothing of good or evil. Once on the planet, Selena dared not turn back, though she found herself in the company of deadly and hostile plant life, monstrous carnivores, and the strange savage who was to lead her through a dream—and a nightmare—in search of the Tree that is All Things.

Turn this book over for
second complete novel

THE
ANYTHING
TREE

JOHN RACKHAM

AN ACE BOOK

Ace Publishing Corporation
1120 Avenue of the Americas
New York, N.Y. 10036

ONE

SELENA ASH was whistling to herself. It was not a tune, but just the soft sibilance of preoccupation as she carefully stripped herself of artifice and pretense. Away into storage went her shimmer-silk absurdity of a dress, the jewel-studded shoes and the expensive but pointless knicknacks; tissues and pin-prick tweaking cleaned away the hectic bloom of cosmetics and false hair; she used cream to eradicate the last traces, and it was all done without any thought. Her mind was elsewhere. Around her, the versatile little space-coupe pursued its set course. There was no hurry; she had more than four days. The mad rush of butterfly brainlessness which spelled out fun for the idle rich on the paradise continent Shangri-La of the playground planet of Tau Ceti III dwindled into her past. She buttoned herself into a white papertex coverall, put her feet into sandals, and went back up the ladder to the control room, not because there was anything to control—the auto mechanisms handled that—but simply because it was where she felt organized.

And she might need the services of the computer to help her with a problem or two. She settled into her seat, cast a routine eye over the dials assembled—blinked—and looked again. She felt an icy chill at her stomach. There was something wrong, something so blatantly wrong that, for a moment, she couldn't accept it. The read-out figure for time of arrival stood at a few minutes over four hours, which was monstrous! She spent a second going over her take-off procedure. Lift-off had been automatic and all clear. In that interval she had preprogrammed for her destination and set the relay switch to kick in the warp as soon as she was clear of the planetary field. That had all happened.

Her program had been for Luna Base, well over a week's journey even at this light-bending speed. She had been flying this little space-coupe or one like it for the past five of her twenty-five years, and it was just not possible that she could have made such a mistake. There were other things wrong, too. She drew a deep and steadying breath and did the

5

first thing one must always do in doubt—stop everything and take stock. She hit the manual dewarp, shivered through the instant of nausea, then eyed the glowing screens which gave her several pictures of vast expanses spotted with stars.

"Now, then," she murmured, and started by pushing down on the interlock. It was already hard down, as it should be. The interlock is the last button one pushes, when everything is set up and smoothly rolling. Then, should anything fail, the interlock throws everything out and screams for attention. It wasn't that. But there is, also, an interlock cancel button, and that, too, was down—which in theory was impossible. She peered closely at it and tugged. It rose sluggishly, leaving a thin layer of some kind of cement.

"Oh, very tricky!" she congratulated someone as yet unknown. Stick a layer of gum on the cancel, press it home, and there you are. No matter what someone else does, no matter what goes wrong, there will be no alarm—neat, simple and deadly. A cold fury began to stir in her mind. Blaming herself was just part of it. She had found it necessary to play the part of an empty-headed social butterfly, and one couldn't do that *and* openly own a ship that was stiff with crafty protective devices and unorthodox equipment. She had set her watchogs in abeyance; she deserved this sabotage, or whatever it was. But who was responsible? Belatedly she remembered that she hadn't eliminated *all* her guards. There was one, a spy-eye. She touched certain switches on the computer, and a side-screen lit up to give her a picture of a young man about her own age, a handsome —perhaps overhandsome—fair young man with a forelock of bright yellow hair, laughing eyes, and very white teeth. She knew him. It was Pierre Lacoste, only son of a wealthy manufacturer of domestic robot equipment. She wondered whether he would know enough to be able to gimmick her ship. Before she could decide, the spy-record stuttered and shifted to another picture, this time of a taller man of the same age. He was lean and satirical, dark-haired, and self-consciously tough, and she knew him also. The man was Robin Delmar, the current hero and star of the jet-boat set, winner of just about every event in the known Galaxy that involved rockets or jets.

"Well, now," she breathed, halting her electronic stoolpigeon. "There's something, by God!" She took her time reviewing what she knew of the two people involved. Together they might just possibly possess enough knowledge to monkey with the ship. Both of them owned and flew their own ships, superficially the same as this one. It was possible but unlikely unless she could think of some reason why. Pierre and Robin and she had been a merry-making trio for some time. Both men had made the expected and routine passes at her and missed. It was part of her art that she could fend off such men without offending them; and they were friendly rivals. But it was nothing more than that, she would swear. She would stake her life that neither man believed her to be anything more than the gay daredevil daughter of Conway Ash—a somebody in reflected glory, for Conway Ash, as chief scientific advisor to the United Planets Office of Technological Strategy, was a force in his own right—but in herself just another rich playgirl.

Stake my life, she mused over her own thought. She might have to do just that, if either of them had found out what she really was, and why. She put the thought away, determined to come back to it only if driven. Assume, then, that Pierre and Robin had gimmicked her ship somehow— for what? The immediate and appropriate answer came back—a joke—and it fitted. If that pair had anything at all in common it was a hilarious (they thought) sense of the absurd. She shook her head wryly, her fury abating somewhat. She spent another moment fitting herself into their viewpoint, then touched another control on her computer, which was not the standard model it appeared to be, but had refinements known only to her and the experts who had installed it.

"Definition," she stated. "Tracer. For your purpose a tracer is any contrivance or device which can be lodged in or on a ship or person such that it will generate a signal detectable at a distance and thus enable its location to be pinpointed by some other appropriate device. Understood?"

The blink signal came up instantly, and she shifted to another button. "Inspect this ship now—thoroughly, inside and out—and contents, including me, for signs of a tracer, and then report."

The answer was thirty-five seconds in coming, which surprised her. The answer itself surprised her even more.

"Four extraneous objects," the computer reported, "match

the given definition. All are broadcasting powerful and continuous signals on the uhf waveband. One has been incorporated into the ship radio console, the others are attached to the hull on the outside. Locations—"

"Never mind, we'll get to that later." She cut the report off and shook her head. "Four? My, my, that doesn't sound like Pierre and Robin. The plan is fine: monkey with my course computer, strand me somewhere, then come dashing to the rescue—the fools! But *four* separate tracers?" She gave up that thought and went back to her spy-eye to try again, more from curiosity than anything else. She got another shock—more faces. The first one was gross and barely human—a fleshy gargoyle of a man with a nose and chin to batter down any obstacle, a craggy brow overshadowing two black eyes, and a mouth that had no lips at all. The next was as different as could be imagined. It was a mature and controlled woman with a face like an underworld madonna—sculptured and flawless—and jet-black hair framed by a glossy helmet. That face could charm away a man's senses—like a snake. Selena ran those two again.

"Those I have never seen before," she breathed. "I couldn't possibly forget a pair like that. God knows how they come to be in cahoots with Pierre and Robin, but the four tracers now begin to make a little more sense. Still, they surely weren't so naïf as to believe that they could toss me lightyears into the unknown and then find me on the tail of a uhf tracer!" The answer to that one was obvious, once she saw it. One of them had preprogrammed a rendezvous, and then gimmicked the course computer so that her program was void. But there had to be more.

"I get to where they have planned and dewarp; that's all right. But then I take a fast look around, realize something has gone wrong, and—so, they must have fixed something else, to stop me from doing just that. Let's see just what, shall we?"

She swung her chair out of the way, grasped at quicktwist bolt-heads, loosened them, and swung out the entire front casing of the course computer. Her anger was seeping back, not at the joke which had been played on her, but at the posture she would now have to adopt because of it. If she went ahead and used her skills to get out of their childish trap, bang went her false front as Selena Ash, brainless butterfly. And it had cost her time and trouble to set up. On the other hand, if she stayed in character and just sat there, helpless and afraid, waiting to be picked up—but what about those two vultures she had seen who were also in on it?

She pulled open a drawer and fished for tools, clicked on a tiny pencil-torch, peered within at the works—and felt another chill. There were the neat rows of second-order relays. Seven of them were tip-tilted to various settings and neatly disconnected from the panel controls so that they couldn't be altered. The pattern was not immediately obvious but she could discover it later. What chilled her right now was a small aluminum capsule that was patch-wired into the warp-out relays. That innocent-looking tube had markings on it, but even without those she would have recognized it for what it was, because she had seen things like it before. The picture burned in her mind. The course computer would run to its completed setting, relays would close, others would open—and that small but deadly destruct module would explode—and that would be the last useful work that computer, or that ship, would ever do. She felt cold sweat break out on her when she realized that if she had not dewarped on the emergency manual control, she would be dead now.

She looked at it for a long while, making herself think. Less and less did this feel like Pierre and Robin. Fools they might be, but this kind of senseless and dangerous destruction was not in their picture. Perhaps it fitted the other pair, though, and that only made the mystery more confusing. At length she backed away and returned to the drawer for more tools. She took long bits and blades and very delicately cut loose the little bomb. With that done, she thought a bit more.

The false front was finished, that much was obvious. Sexy Selena would never have been able to find that bomb or recognize it, much less remove it. But it couldn't be allowed to rest there. Whatever the score was, she had to find out just what was going on. The obvious way to do that was to go wherever it was they had planned her to go, and see what was laid on. That called for a little preparation and thought. First she made a careful note of the relay settings, and, with spider tongs, adjusted the board from below until she could reconnect and make everything good. Then she closed the console again, put away her tools, checked that everything was in order, hit the warp switch and held her breath.

Apart from the customary instant of nausea as the ship leaped into its interrupted path, nothing happened. She breathed again, buttoned down the interlock, and then applied herself once more to the computer's special circuitry.

"First," she said, "you will check right through the ship, looking for anything—any other extraneous devices or anomalies—anything!"

That drew a highly reassuring blank. "Now," she said more easily, "extrapolate from the course settings and identify destination. Read it out for me."

The shimmering blue figures came up almost at once and didn't mean a thing. She scowled, shaking her head.

"Halfway to nowhere. Celestial reference chart, please!"

The tabulated data dissolved, gave way to a schematic star map with a small blue winker to indicate the spot she was headed for. She eyed it, shook her head again. "Any further data?" The picture stayed steady.

"That's it," she sighed. "And what a waste of time that was. 'Way out in the wilds—uncharted space at least thirty lights away from Tau Ceti, and more than twice that from anywhere known."

She cancelled the display, glanced at the ETA figure, saw just under four hours, and nodded. There was a glint in her gray eyes that would have astonished her recent cronies.

"Time for a meal," she said, "and a nap. And then I set up a few odd things on my own hook. If somebody really is trying to kill me, I want to know who, and why, and maybe to register an objection or two."

TWO

SHE AWOKE with fifteen minutes to spare before her deadline, just long enough to sweep the fog from her thoughts and be ready as the passing seconds counted down. Her instructions were all keyed in and ready. The arrival warning bonged sonorously, there came that instant inside-out feeling, star-fields lit the screens, and in the same second her computer was gobbling a mass of data, processing it, and getting ready to go. She read the situation with grim delight. Luck! There was a small sun and planetary system no more than four-tenths of a light away. And there was one small, solid, metal, power-emitting object much closer than that—as she had expected. She saw this all in one fast survey, then, as fast as her fingers could move, she aimed for that insignificant sun-system and buttoned for a hop. Sliced seconds later there was a raving glow in her forward screens, and it called for hasty but sure adjustments while she spun into orbit about it. That done she sat back.

"All right, whoever you are," she challenged. "Let's see how long it takes you to sort your tracers from this mush. Try and find me, if you can!"

She felt sure they would, but not immediately, and that was as much as she had hoped for. She now had a breathing space in which to dig a better hiding place. She got busy with scanner and analysis; her radio was on to listen to the blanketing wash of static from the unnamed sun. Whoever was in that ship was hardly likely to broadcast his presence yet. Before anything else, he was going to have to think up some reason why she was not just hung there helpless. And that might make him pause a little. Meanwhile she went over the data on this sun's planets in the hope of finding somewhere to stop. She did not fancy being attacked in space. Her ship was special, and versatile far beyond its routine appearance, but it wasn't that good. On the ground she could even the odds quite a bit. And she was lucky again. One of the slow-circling planets, the

11

second out, looked promising. Indeed, as she went over the data again, it was more than that.

"Very nice!" She approved. "Sub-tropical primitive, slightly smaller than Earth, acceptable atmosphere and temperatures—might have been made to order." She got busy again, but not rashly. Distant figures and analyses give only a part of the picture. A lushly welcoming planet might turn out to be anything but that on closer acquaintance, and this place was completely off the charts. She slid into a thousand-mile orbit and gave the detection complexes another workout. The acceptability still stood up, so she studied the surface and selected her spot with care and an eye to the questions of cover and defense. There were many minor landmasses, and one enormous one lying athwart the equator. At its northern tip was a beaky promontory, a long flat plain backed by rugged mountains, with dense forest on either side of them.

"That," she decided, "will do me very well. Down among the trees, with the plain in front, the mountains at my back, sea on either side, and let them come and get me—if they can!"

She went down, using the ship's extra-powerful grav-fields to check her fall right up to the last minute, and then settled stern-first among the trees with the absolute minimum of scorching and burning to leave marks for others to notice. And then, with a sigh, she was able to sit back once more. She had an hour in which the sensitive sniffing systems would subject every indrawn molecule to severe scrutiny and assess it for danger. That particular analytical plant, too, was not standard on a ship like this, but Selena by now had abandoned all shadow of pretense of being standard. Whoever it was who had initiated this round of fun-and-games would soon find that he had taken on more than he realized. She reviewed her strategy. They had been laying for her, that much was proven. She had no idea why, but that could wait. Her evasion had been fast, but she was not kidding herself that she had escaped without detection. They had seen her arrive. The ship's bulk itself, even without their tracers, would have rung that bell. But she had warped out again, and that might throw them for a while, especially as they had every right to assume that she would be helpless.

She pondered it. They would have to assume that the bomb damage was not as total as they had planned—but that she *was* damaged, partly crippled. Therefore, in logic, she would have to find landfall somewhere close—which she had done. They would come to look; but she had time to listen to the thousand and one small noises of the surrounding forest re-establishing itself after her arrival. There was time to admire the view in her screens. The forward cameras had two pictures: on one there was a waving mass of treetops, and beyond those a mountain range, purple with distance and, in one or two instances, white-crested with snow; on the other she saw more treetops, a glimpse of a silvery yellow beach, and the rolling sea. The stern viewers showed her a quiet wilderness of tree trunks and a profusion of tangled bushes and creepers heavy with multicolored blooms.

"This is quite a place," she declared. "If the life systems check out—and that is quite a big *if*, of course—this is quite a find! Might even be worth laying claim to!"

The idea amused her for a while. Because of a number of nasty legal hassles over rights to the first few desirable planets that had been discovered, there were several ironclad statutes on the books, one of which effectively stopped any whole-planet claims by individuals or minorities. The first person to locate, establish and record the existence of a new planet had an inalienable right to claim one square mile of its surface—any square mile—as his property, to dispose of as he saw fit. But that was all.

That line of speculation filled the time until the life systems yielded up their verdict. She studied the data carefully. Everything was in the green, except for two items which were underlined for her attention. One was an inconclusive harmless measurement of longwave electromagnetic radiation of unknown origin. The other was an activation analysis of certain complex organic molecules common to the local botanical spectrum; it was not harmful either, but unusual and unexplained.

She frowned, went back to the longwave electromagnetic radiation, then clicked her tongue in chagrin. One might as well try to measure the temperature with a foot rule! Of course one wouldn't expect a chemical analysis to recogize radio! But why was it on the longwave band? It had to be local, from the surface. Longwaves could not push through the ionosphere. Maybe that was the reason—so that no one outside would get them! She turned on her radio, which was still yielding hushed static, and there it was, on the tell-tale—a winking green neon that said something was coming in. She made adjustments and tuned down, and suddenly there was a drawly male voice in the middle of a sentence.

"—liked that. I did, too. Here's another one you're going to like, by a feller named Strauss. It's called Morning Papers, which can't mean a thing to you, because you never saw a morning paper—nor yet an evening one, for that matter—but who cares about that? Here it comes, now," and the slow voice, an outrageous caricature of hillbilly drawl, went away and on came the classic Strauss waltz.

Selena felt the first faint twinge of unreality. She stared at her radio in frank unbelief, and tapped it just to make sure. Rational explanation eluded her completely. That someone else had found this planet ahead of her and had landed wasn't so hard to take. She had considered that very possibility, although in a slightly different context. But that such a predecessor would refrain from making contact in the normal way, by uhf or a visual signal and would then broadcast, like this, as if to an audience—on longwave was incredible. She put her thumb on the transmit switch and hesitated uneasily. So many unlikely things had happened that she wondered if maybe the trouble was in herself.

"Curiouser and curiouser," she quoted wryly, and managed a smile. "I'm sure I was perfectly normal when I took off!" It was something of a shock to count up the hours and realize just how recently that was. Then, bracing herself, she pushed the button and drew breath.

"This is space-coupe K.T. one-oh-four, out of Luna and Shangri-La; Selena Ash, owner-pilot, speaking. Who are you? Identify!"

She repeated it, then released the button and waited. The Strauss lilt went on. There was neither reply nor any sign she had been heard. She shrugged it off, getting a little tired of trying to answer questions without data. Whoever it was, she could try again later. She had other things to attend to, such as the four tracers. The module in her radio was simple, she could deal with that at once and did so. It had been patched in and was a standard broad-channel whistler which told her nothing at all. She crushed it and tossed the fragments into the disposal. The outside ones would need something a little more elaborate.

She tried her tool drawer again, took a small satchel and loaded it with what she hoped would be enough and slung it over her shoulder. Then she got out a small beamer and grip and buckled it about her hips, smiling her wry smile as she realized just how wide-eyed either Robin or Pierre would be if they could see this—or would they? Her smile became a cold menace as she reflected that she had not yet properly evaluated the possibility that those two apparently innocent young men may have taken her for a very fast ride! She didn't want to add in that value, because it would mean she had lost what was possibly her biggest advantage.

She went out and down the gangway ladder, debating in her mind whether to rig it with a few safety precautions. Then she glanced around at the peaceful greenery and decided against it. She had no intention of going very far away, just far enough to be able to get at those tracers. And she was quite confident of her ability to handle anything obvious that might come up. There was a circle of scorched vegetation around the base of the ship which gave her a clear walkway until she could come to one of the landing feet. She saw the thing she was after where a strut crossed and merged with the hull. A small chunk of dull silver metal clung limpetlike to the nook between strut and hull; it was the sort of thing no one would notice without having it pointed out. There was another on the other side and one right under the stern, by the steering venturi. They were slick, professional jobs, not at all in keeping with Pierre and Robin.

She rummaged in her satchel and brought out a thick tube of plastic nine inches long. Into one end she fitted an alloy chisel bit; the other end carried a knurled band, which she twisted while gripping the shaft of the tube. She twisted hard, and the tube grew lengthwise as it shrank in girth, telescoping out, longer and longer, but still rigid. She aimed it upwards and kept on squeezing until it was long enough to reach the offending object. Now —unless it was welded on, and she didn't think they'd had time for that—she was going to chip it off. Taking careful aim, she gripped both hands, lowered, and then jabbed upwards strongly. After another solid jab she thought she could see the beginnings of a crack and nodded. It was epoxy-resin, most probably. She shifted her position slightly, took another swing—and the thing flew apart with a flare and explosion which deafened and blinded her for a moment. She felt the quick heat of it on her face, and the jerk as the explosion whipped her tool out of her grasp and out of sight among the bushes.

She stood still, her ears jangling and her vision full of dark spots, then shook her head grimly. Very nasty—someone was playing very rough indeed. This was not *her* playmates, at all. Suppose she had, somehow, climbed up there to remove that thing! As soon as she could see and hear well enough she stooped, ducked under her ship and out the other side; this time she wasted no motions on delicacy. Drawing her beamer, she laid her wrist alongside the hull, took aim, shut her eyes and fired. Once more there was a bright flash and a thunderclap explosion, but this time she was ready for it and untroubled.

"I think," she murmured, "we'll leave him just one. After all, I'd hate to have him miss me, after all the trouble he's gone to."

She crouched and passed under her ship again to where she had started from, and tried to recall which way her long chisel had flown—not far, surely. Reliving the moment and remembering, she worked out a direction, and started off cautiously to look for it, parting the bushes and taking care not to get confused. Three steps got her to more bushes, and then, as she eased through them and stood, she was looking across a small clearing, an open space about six or seven yards across. There by the foot of a tree, was her chisel. But it wasn't just there. It was held firmly by the man who had picked it up.

THREE

HER FIRST impression was of bulk pared down to the precise needs of efficiency. He was over six feet tall, but the relaxed yet alert way he stood and the shift and play of the long ropy muscles in his forearm as he turned over her rod to inspect it, modified that first impression into a more accurate assessment of power, not just size. He belonged here, in some indefinable yet positive way, as fittingly as the tree against which he stood. She took another breath to study him in detail: the broad sloping shoulders, filled-out chest, lean waist, strong legs, leather-tanned skin, but most of all his neck and the set of his head. A god of the greenwood— the term came unbidden and unwanted. In her instinctive rejection of it she drew her beamer and leveled it at him.

Then she was able to take time for closer study still because he seemed totally unaware of her presence. His blond hair, very pale and washed out by exposure, hung in a rude shock to his shoulders. About his hips, either as a ragged belt or a skimpy loincloth, was a band of curiously woolly stuff, some kind of fiber, which served to support a bright bladed knife and a curious pouch. Her eyes narrowed at the latter. It contained soil. From it sprang a slim green stem with tiny regular leaves; the stem climbed up and over his chest, around his left shoulder and then vanished into the thicket of his hair. Just beyond him, leaning against the tree, was a seven foot spear of yellow-brown wood, the final foot of it shining metal like his knife. Was he a native—a wild man? She couldn't quite believe that, not by the way he was studying her chisel. Not when he gripped it experimentally and began twisting the knurled end, so that it began to contract again.

The moment stretched. What does one say in a case like this? Then she received a shock as her eyes again followed that twisting, climbing stem to where it lost itself in his hair —and saw a big and bright blue eye peering out. An eye? She caught her breath again as she realized that it was no more than a flower head, that only *seemed* to be staring at her. But it was enough to sharpen her mood. She stepped one more pace to be clear of the bushes and waved the beamer for reassurance.

"Hold it!" she advised firmly. "Hold it right there!" He didn't move as much as a single muscle. "I don't know whether you can understand me or not, but don't do anything fast. Just turn, slowly." He turned quite easily and with no sign of surprise whatever. His head came around first, then the rest of him, and she met a calm stare from the brightest and yet most impersonal eyes she had ever seen, uncannily like the one-eyed look of the blue flower. If there was an expression at all on his face it was of guarded curiosity.

"This is a weapon," she warned, waving the beamer again. "Who are you?"

After a moment for seeming thought he said, "Call me Joe. Better put that weapon away out of your hand, ma'am." His voice was a soft drawl, seeming to drop the words halfway between them. The same drawl she had heard on the longwave with the music.

"You're civilized! Why the primitive savage bit?"

"Why not? Who's to notice? Better put away your hardware."

"Why should I? What are you afraid of?"

"Not me. I live here. It's you. All the time you're clutching that thing you're feeling aggressive. That's a reflex. You can't help it. But the plants around these parts are sensitive to that kind of thing. They don't like it a bit. I'm doing all I can to comfort 'em, else they'd have had you long ago. Better put it up. I can't hold 'em still forever."

He was very calm, almost indifferent, nor had he made another move after facing her. His bland superiority irritated her.

"You're out of your mind. You're masterminding plants! Do you really expect me to believe that?"

"Don't expect you to believe nothing," he said, with what could have been a small smile tugging at the corner of his mouth. "Guess you're the kind as has to be shown. Just don't blame it on me, that's all. It's all right, Friendly, you can relax!" He moved his right hand slowly across his chest to reach the inquisitive blue flower on his shoulder, to spread his palm, still slowly, and cover that bright blue eye.

Selena saw his hand curl into a cup—and shrieked as lashing twigs fastened on her ankles, her wrist, curled about her waist, stooped down to tangle in her hair—twigs with thorns, stringy and strong twigs that gripped and tore and contracted with pressure. Needles of pain erupted from her skin where the sharp-toothed thorns bit. Pressure constricted her breast, her waist, slimp ropes dragged at her legs until she began to totter, and the more she struggled the harder the coils tightened, until panic blossomed in her heart.

"Now stop!" His voice suddenly had the edge of authority. "You been shown, now? How much more do you want? Quit struggling!"

His scorn sliced through her panic, biting deeper than plant's venom. Breathlessly she held still, feeling the slow glide and coiling of more ropy twigs. "Better. Just hold still, and pay attention to me, I can't do it all by myself, you have to help. First off, drop that fool weapon, you hear?" She unclenched her hand and heard the beamer thud to the turf. "That's fine! Now, comb the fright out of your mind. You have to feel friendly, real friendly, to the plants and me and everything. Go on, feel friendly. Pretty flowers! Nice, kind plants. You didn't mean them any harm. You *like* plants! Go on, do it!"

She couldn't—not at first. The inescapable awareness of physical helplessness wouldn't allow it. There were tightly constricting bands of living fiber about her body and a thousand small scratches burned painfully on her skin. But she did realize, as she held fearfully still, that the snaky plants were still, too.

"Me and Friendly can stop 'em," he pointed out, still with quiet scorn, "but we can't make 'em back up, not while you're boiling like that!"

I'll get you, she vowed. *Later!* And then, swallowing and making a great effort, she took charge of herself; she willed herself to feel kindly towards the ropy green horrors—no, that wouldn't do—towards the pleasant and pretty plants which were caressing her to show their delight at her presence. *Nice plants, pretty bushes, such beautiful flowers and leaves*—it was almost the hardest thing she had ever done. It was ridiculous, offensive to common sense and destructive to dignity, but she made the silly phrases form in her mind and repeated them. She felt the capturing strands loosen, little by little. Fervently she filled her mind with beneficent thoughts towards all vegetation, and the snaking strands began to uncurl, to withdraw and to leave her free. That sensation was a strange and creepy one, but she buried that thought deep under a flood of sickly praise and flattery until the last leathery bond had shifted away and she was free.

Aloof and superior, he was still standing there watching her. She moved a step, catching her breath at the instant agony from a host of scratches. Another, and she stooped like someone with rheumatism to take up her beamer. In that moment she caught sight of her hips and legs, and the once-neat coverall was a shredded and rapidly dissolving ruin, melting even as she stared at it; it was rotting away under the sticky green ichor of the venomous plants. That, somehow, was more than she could stand—on top of the other humiliations. She seized the weapon, intending to run clear of the horrors behind her, and then she would make him—but she never got so far as deciding just what punishment would be fitting. It was as if a mighty padded fist slammed down on the top of her head, drove her down into the ground and into darkness.

She came back to consciousness flat on her back, with a sour-acid taste in her mouth and the instant intuition that it would be unwise to move. The assurance of pain was very close. The ceiling looked familiar; it was her own. She stirred, became aware that she was stretched out on her own bunk and covered by the thin foil of an insulex blanket; the pain wasn't as bad as she had dreaded. Half sitting, turning her head, she could see through the half-open cabin door into the control room. This was the upper-deck cabin, just big enough to take a cot and necessaries; it was the one she used when on a solo flight, so that she could be near enough to the controls to get there fast, if necessary. The living cabins proper were one deck down. Why had he carried her all the way up here? She sat all the way up, disturbed by the implications of that thought; and there he was, Joe the non-savage, seated at her panel, listening curiously to her radio, so muted that all she could hear was a buzzing murmur. Disquiet grew in her mind as she realized she was quite nude under the crackly foil blanket.

"Don't try anything violent," he advised, without turning his head and without threat. "Those plant scratches carry a venom—not lethal, but it can be a pesty itch for a while. You have a real cute diagnoster unit here. I used it to whip up an injection for you that should take off the worst, but you have to give it time. Just hold still. I have coffee ready. I'll get it." He rose and went silently away on bare feet, posing her a little problem. Where before had she seen a man move like that? It was not catlike, not at all tigerish, but flowing. Male ballet dancers—that was it. Then he was back with a self-heat carton for her and one for himself. He settled on the far edge of her cot.

"That's doped," he said, handing it to her. "Make you feel better fast. Mine's just to be sociable. How d'you feel?"

"I'm fairly comfortable." She sat up, grasping the thin foil and sipping the welcome warmth. "I suppose I ought to thank you."

"No matter. That venom, like I said, isn't lethal. You get enough of it in your system and it acts like alcohol—puts you down. That's what it's for. So the plants can take their time about tearing you apart and combining the remains with the soil. Don't mean anything; it's just their way of living."

"I see!" She repressed a shudder at the mental images which came. "I owe you my life, then. Are all the local plants like that?"

"More or less—all I know about. They don't do a thing if you keep calm and friendly. Sort of protective device, you could call it. Sensitive to emotional fields, I reckon."

Selena became sensitively aware that she was naked under the thin foil. "I'm grateful, of course, but was it absolutely necessary to take my clothes off?"

"Weren't none to take off," he retorted blandly. "That's one more bit you need to know. The local life is savage with any strange molecules. So far as I know, they bend their teeth on bright metal, like T-alloys, and one or two of the plastics, but they sure destroy anything else they don't like. That's why I wear this stuff. It's a local fiber."

"I see," she said again, feeling inadequate, and once more irritated, because it was not her pattern to feel diminished by anyone else, least of all a man. "You seem to be able to manage quite well."

"I live here," he said, as if that explained everything. "Been looking over your ship, ma'am. It's a dilly. Sure have been some improvements since—" he hesitated there, went off on another tack. "You seem to be in some kind of trouble, ma'am. Don't want to push it, but have you any plans in mind?"

"Trouble? Plans?" She put the carton aside. "You seem to know a lot about it?"

"Used my head a little, that's all. You had radio tracers stuck to your hull. You got rid of two, left one."

"You were watching me?"

"Right! You came down in a hellova hurry and then kept quiet. It all adds up this way. Somebody stuck a tail on you, and you were on the run. You scratched some of the tail, but left some, too. Means you want to be found, you maybe aim to put up some kind of resistance. By your board there, the enemy is right on to it and will be homing in any time."

"How long was I unconscious?"

"About twenty minutes. I figure it will take those birds up there a while yet to work out what they're going to do. Plenty of time for you to take off and blow!"

"I have no intention of taking off! Why do you imagine I came down here in the first place?"

"No idea, ma'am. I just want you to up-ship and get."

"Why? What's it to you?"

"This is my planet. I like it just the way it is."

"Your planet? *Your* planet? Who d'you think you are, anyway?"

It was as if an impenetrable shutter descended before his eyes and face and he went away, not physically but in some mental fashion. "I sort of figured you'd take it like that," he said softly and rose; he turned and was almost gone from sight before she could find voice.

"Wait! Stop! Where d'you think you're going?"

"Away. Out of the way. This is nothing of my affair."

She scrambled from the bunk, clutching at the foil cover, forcing unpleasant words into her mouth. "No, don't go. Look, Joe, I need your help!"

"Nothing I can do."

"But there is. Listen. I don't know who those people are up there or why they are after me. You've seen their style, the way those tracers were boobied with detonite. They play rough. Now, if I take off, I'm wide open. If you know anything about ships at all, you know that. This isn't an armored ship; I wouldn't stand a chance. This way, down on the ground, they have to land and come at me on the level. At least I'll have a chance to see who they are and maybe find out what this is all about."

"You don't need my help to sit here and wait for that."

"But I'm not going to sit here. I'm going out there. I'll

leave the ship sealed so they won't be able to get in—it's designed for that—and hide out somewhere near, and watch. Honestly, I don't know what this is all about, and I need to know, and that's the only way I can think of. And, for that, I need your help. You know this terrain!"

He stood blank-faced a long while, as the curious flower eye peered at her from over his shoulder. Then he stirred, and shook his head.

"All right, I reckon that's the best way to settle this thing. Come on, then!"

FOUR

SHE MADE a step then realized the state she was in. "Oh! What'll I wear?"

"Can't help you there, ma'am. Less you have something made of metal—maybe that foil would make a kind of wrap."

"Hardly. Besides, it would be visible for miles. Oh, I know!" and still clutching the inadequate foil sheet around her she scurried down one deck to her living space and dug into her wardrobe locker to produce a dress she had worn only once and never expected to wear again. It was made entirely of inch-diameter titanium rings cunningly inter-linked—some limp-brained designer's notion of a chain-mail shirt, she believed. She had felt an utter fool wearing it the first time, and she didn't feel much happier about it now, but at least it would serve.

She went back up, to find him listening at the radio once more. "Are they sending?" she asked, and he wound up the volume so that she could hear.

". . . if you can. Reply if you can. This is G.R. six-oh-five calling ground. Are you reading me? Reply if you can, please!"

"Sounds friendly," he commented, cutting the sound. "Mean anything?"

"Yes indeed. G.R. six-oh-five—that's Robin Delmar's ship. She's very fast and fancy. He's a jet ace. I thought he was a friend of mine, but now I don't know; I'm not so sure.

Certainly not sure enough to go waltzing up there and be blown apart. No, hold on while I fix a thing or two."

He stood by the down hatch and let her get on with it, apparently much more interested in her tool bag than in what she was doing. She set certain mechanisms into watchfulness, established a code signal, caught up a tiny portable sender and her beamer, and buckled both to the metal belt of her dress. He, apparently, hadn't even noticed it; that piqued her a little. She was ill-accustomed to being ignored.

"This is quite a gadget, this expanding rod," he murmured, turning it over in his lean fingers. "New to me."

"New to almost anyone," she said. "You've seen a pair of lazy tongs? That molecular structure is the same. Lateral pressure creates a linear deformation in the structure. It's handy. Not on the open market yet, though."

"Yeah." He dropped it back in her satchel and lifted his head. "You ready? I'll show you a place to hide."

"Just a minute." She was beginning to catch nuances in his tone and attitude. "I don't mean that you shall show me somewhere—and then decamp!"

"This is none of my affair," he repeated stolidly. "I don't aim to get involved any more than I have to. You fight your own battles!"

"Now see here!" She sharpened her words angrily. "I am Selena Ash. My father is Conway Ash, chief advisor to the U.P. Office of Technological Strategy. You must have heard of him. You know he is a very important man. If anything should happen to me, he will want to know why, and who, and heads will roll. On the other hand, if I can tell him that you helped me . . ." She was talking to his back. He went down and away so fast that she had to scramble and run to catch him just at the head of the gangway.

"You're a coward," she snapped, and he halted easily.

"No, ma'am, just a disinterested bystander. Even if you are all you say—and there's no proof—your father can't do anything for me or to me."

"But I can!" She had a sudden and vindictive inspiration. "You had better be interested. If and when I get away from here—or someone gets away from here—there'll be talk, and you won't be able to stop it. This is a nice pleasant planet—highly desirable. The word will get around. People will come here in droves, thousands of them. I promise you that!"

There was no visible change in his stone-wall look, but she could feel the change in tension, and she knew she had him. The blue flower head suddenly ducked back out of sight into his hair.

"You're really twisting my arm, now, ma'am. Reckon I'll have to do what you want." Startlingly, he grinned, and it was like an animal showing its teeth. "What do you have in mind?"

His immediate capitulation took her off balance for a moment. Then she said, "Let's get out of the ship and away first—somewhere safe. I'll have to play it by ear from there. Lead on!"

Minutes later she stood shoulder to shoulder with him among the thick bushes that had so recently tried to destroy her in their mindless fashion, and held her portable sender close to her face. Deliberately she whistled into it the first bars of Beethoven's Fifth and watched as the gangway drew itself up and the exit hatch swung shut.

"So much for that," she said. "It's up to you, now."

"Right!" He spun and went away at what looked like an easy stride, but which made her stretch her long legs to keep up.

"What about your ship and that longwave broadcast?" she panted, and he nodded without pausing.

"That's first. I have things to button up. Won't take a minute. Then we hide out. We have time. I know the spot."

He knew the area, too, she realized as he led her a stiff course in and out between massive boles and through riotous undergrowth. He went up and over the irregular ground, occasionally leaping a small stream and striding as easily as if the way were a broad, smooth boulevard. Within five minutes she had no breath for questions and in another five she was sweating. However ridiculous the chain-mail dress might be, it was light and extremely well-ventilated. She slogged on grimly.

Eventually they reached a small clearing, and he halted on the edge of it and waited for her. She heard the faint lilt of an orchestra playing yet another Strauss waltz.

"You stay right here," he commanded. "I won't be a minute."

"No!" she panted in instant objection. "What are you going to do?"

"Turn off the music, for one thing. Friendly's folks will have to get along without it for a little while. Don't want nosy strangers hearing it and coming to snoop. Hold this."

He thrust the spear at her. "No, wait," she protested. "Can't I come with you?"

His bleak stare went oddly with his gleaming smile. "You don't trust me, I know. Why should you? I don't trust you, neither. Once I shut off that music and do a couple of things —well, you can't see my ship from here, and when I'm through you'll never be able to find it. You, nor anyone else. That's the way I want it, ma'am; that's how it's going to be. You can twist my arm just so far. After that it just breaks off in your hand!"

"But"—she objected uneasily—"you're going to leave me all alone, here, by myself."

"You're among friends. Nothing to be scared of, not that you strike me as the nervous kind. Anyhow, Friendly's folks will let you know should any danger happen by."

The last she saw of him was his broad back disappearing through the further wall of bushes ablaze with scarlet blooms. She would have said, herself, that she was not the nervous type, but her recent experience with predatory vegetation had planted a seed of uneasiness in her. She gripped his spear, but was a lot happier at the thought of the beamer on her hip. Standing still, she had time to cool off a little. Properly, she should have been wearing something under it and the bare metal wasn't very comfortable, but the mere thought of something close and clinging made her sweat all over again. The distant music stopped, leaving a gap in the sound scene.

A phrase of his came back—friendly flowers. The way he said it gave it the status of a pet name, almost of someone called Friendly—and his folks. She became aware that the quiet glade was ringed with wide-eyed blue flowers like the one he wore. They were all turned her way, staring at her; there could be no doubt about it this time. In all that host there should have been a few at least that were turned some other way—but no. And then it burst upon her mind. These were Friendly's folks—relatives! And it seemed that the blue-eyed host nodded gently at her understanding. She felt giddy. *I'm going out of my mind!* she thought, but then she painfully recalled those other plants and their deadly offensive on her. And what had he said? That they were sensitive to emotional fields? It was that peculiar molecule her life-systems analysis had found! The giddy sense of unreality grew. Any moment now, she realized, she would be talking to them and expecting them to answer back, like Alice in Looking-Glass country. To rescue herself from gibbering insanity she turned her attention to the spear in her hand.

It was six feet of light, rigid wood, with regular rings like some kind of bamboo—and then a twelve-inch tip, which was a strange silver-gray metal that she couldn't identify. It started off round and gradually became flattened and pointed, and edged like a razor. But there was something else. She brought it close, but she couldn't see how the metal was jointed to the wood. It just was. It was wood, and then it was metal. A flicker of movement caught her eye. Joe was coming back again with a battered pair of binoculars on a glossy black strap.

"Knew I had these someplace." He held the glasses to show her, then slung the strap over his shoulder. "Been so long, I couldn't recall just where I had 'em cached. Might come handy. Let's go."

"Where to now?" she demanded, returning his spear.

"You'll see. We're going to cast around in a circle now. There's a big rock stump right near where you came down. From the top of that we can see where your friends light and something of what they do."

He led off again, once more at that distance-eating pace so that she had to scramble, and in places, break into a stumbling trot, to keep up. She gathered breath enough for a question, though.

"Joe, tell me—how long have you been living—like this?"

"Never bothered to count the days. It's been a good while. You happen to know the date, off-hand, I could tell you better."

"It's month four, twenty-forty-four. The fifteenth, I think."

"That so? Then it works out about four years and a bit. Useless information, but you're welcome to it."

Four years—her mind chewed on that while her arms, legs and lungs labored to keep up with him over the exacting terrain. A person could go native, or primitive—or mad—in four months in a place like this. But any man who could

27

so thoroughly shrug off civilization and learn to adapt this well had to be something special. Suspicions began to ferment in her mind; she itched to know more. It would have to wait for now, but it wouldn't be forgotten.

"Whoa up," he ordered, all at once. "Pretty soon now we'll be leaving the shrub cover and moving out into the open, then on to bare rock. You need to know one thing—pay heed, now. If and when I say 'Down!', you go down flat. Don't argue, don't waste any time, just hug the ground hard as you can 'till I tell you to stop. Got that?"

"Wouldn't it help for me to know why?"

"No time to explain. Hear that thunder? Sounds like your company is getting all fixed to land. Come on."

The rocks were hot, sandy-brown and rough to her feet. He scrambled over them like a goat, his tan blending well with the background, while she felt as conspicuous as a street lamp on a dark night. And his agility was heartbreaking, especially when she considered that he carried a spear in one hand, while she had both hands free and needed them. The overhead muttering was louder now. They came to a crest of sorts, and he halted, allowing her to catch up and stand beside him.

"See 'em?" he asked, and she looked, putting up a hand to shield her eyes from the sun. Barely visible in the burning blue she saw a slim silver needle.

"Yes, I can see the ship."

"Reckon he'll come down somewhere over that way, out in the open not too far from the trees. That's quite a trick, coming down the way you did, and he probably won't chance it—not having any need to take cover." She dropped her gaze to follow where his long arm pointed, out over the plain and the beach. "Taking cover is something we ought to do, though," he went on. "No sense in asking to be shot at. We—hold it!" Urgency shivered in his voice.

"What?"

"Get set to drop. When I say—when I say—now, down!"

She threw herself down, saw him go down by her side, and slicing the air where they had been standing came a vicious whine like the grandfather of all hornets in a temper. It flicked by—not just one, but many—and they were gone as abruptly as they had come.

"What?" she asked, again, without moving.

"I call 'em arrow birds, only they're not birds at all, but a kind of winged lizard, with feet like razors and beaks like swords. Fool things spot something moving, they take a bead, and just dive straight at 'em. They can't change aim in mid-flight, so all you have to do is wait for the moment, and then duck, and they go right on by."

"Will they be back?"

"Sure, if you wiggle about."

"How big are they, average?"

"About a foot long, nine inches of which is beak—and deadly."

"So," she muttered. "They go right on by, do they? We'll see about that!" and she turned over and sat up, drawing her beamer as she did so, and combing the nearby sky for traces of movement.

FIVE

SHE WAS ready for his protest, but nothing came. He just lay there, quite still, and she didn't know which she hated most, him, or the unknown and as yet unseen arrow birds. She saw them only just in time, three vivid green and orange blurs power-diving out of the blue straight for her head. She aimed and fired with desperate speed and tore the last one apart so close that she was showered with scorched debris and assailed by a vile stench.

"That's all there is." He sat up casually, dusted himself off, and turned toward her. "You're pretty good with that thing. Most I've ever tried is batting at them with my spear. For that you need to be flat up against a vertical. They're stupid, but not so they'll run themselves into a rock."

"Have you ever examined one in detail?"

"Couple of times. Takes patience, but you can sometimes lure 'em to dive and get within reach of a bush. That does it. But I just duck out of the way now. It's no trouble. Friendly can feel them half a mile away. We'd better take cover now. Come on."

He moved over a ledge, dropping to where there was enough overhang to provide a shadow for them to crouch

29

in. The noise was enough to feel on her bare skin now, and she saw the sunlight gleaming from the pencil-slim outline of a space-coupe very like her own as it set down over a raving tail of fire and put it out. Then there was echoing silence. That, she felt sure, was Robin Delmar at the controls. It was his kind of professionalism."

"A neat, clean job," he drawled. "That'd be the jet ace you spoke of, I reckon."

"Yes. I can almost see the markings from here."

"What did you say the registration number was?" he murmured, and she turned to see him hoist his binoculars and peer through them. She saw something more, an oddity that exploded a fire-cracker burst of questions in her mind and to her tongue.

She choked them down and managed to say, "Gut-Ripper, six-oh-five. Can you see it?"

"Try a look yourself." He passed the battered instrument across to her and she put it up as he had done, just to be sure, then fiddled with the focusing adjustment and other things.

"That's it—my friends. I'm pretty sure Pierre will be in there with him, maybe some others."

"You sound sort of mixed up," he said. "Talking about it might help some. It would sure help me, anyway, to know what kind of deal I've been roped into."

"I'm sorry about that," she said, and meant it.

"You have plenty of time to talk. The way he chopped her down, that hull will be too damned hot to get out for close on an hour yet. I'd appreciate whatever you can tell."

"Yes. Well, you'll have heard of Shangri-La, even if you've never been there, yes?"

"I know it. Millionaire's playground. Tau Ceti Three."

"Right. And you'll know the kind of affair, too. Good friends and fun partners, nothing more than that, although both Pierre and Robin would have liked it to go a little deeper, perhaps. Anyway, I got an ethergram that called me back urgently to Luna. I didn't tell anyone, but I suppose there are ways of finding out such things. At any rate, I programmed for Luna, and thought no more about it until I happened to notice—well, that the board didn't tally with my program." She told him the rest of it briefly, and he made no comment at all until she reached the part dealing with the destruct module. Then he grunted.

"I don't blame you for being mixed up, ma'am. Bollixing a courser is one thing—laying tracers, that fits, too. I could pass that off as some kind of practical joke, although I don't care for them, and they ought to be barred in space-craft. But that destruct, and the boobies on the tracers—that's another smell entirely." He stared again at that silent ship away over there. "Somebody seems to want you dead!"

"I've been considering that, of course, but isn't it a bit extreme? I mean, I was never supposed to tamper with the tracers anyway—if a certain party was assuming that the destruct module would be enough to cripple me, the tracers wouldn't come into it."

"That's pretty thin, and it won't hold up in any case. Unless they have changed the design considerably, your courser complex is sitting right on top of your environmental master-board. Did you know that?"

"I suppose I did." She frowned, and then chilled as the implications came to her. "Oh my God!"

"All of that, ma'am. Maybe whoever did it didn't think any more than you, but I wouldn't care to chance my skin on it. Maybe you'd have been able to suit up fast enough, but I wouldn't care to bet on that, either. In the dark, with no air, no power, no tripping-and-closing supply—everything out and dead? I wouldn't care to try it, myself."

There was a long and thoughtful silence between them. Her thinking was severely handicapped by the growing mass of intriguing evidence about him, all the odd twists and quirks of clues that didn't quite add up, and nagged at her when she should have been giving cold and rational consideration to the plight she was in. He stirred suddenly.

"Reckon your friends will bear watching, ma'am. And that hull ought to be cool enough for them to start moving. Soon's they do, we'll take off and beat them back to your ship. That's where they'll make for."

"Yes, of course."

"Thing is to watch *how* they do it. If they just run out the gangway, and then walk away from it, leaving it open, well, that ought to say that they don't mean all that much harm."

"But we have already assumed otherwise, surely?"

"No. We figured *somebody* was playing rough, sure, but let's not be too quick to decide—that's the gangway now!"

She lay still, watching as a tiny and distant sliver of metal came out and down to the ground. Then two gaudily clad figures came into sight and tramped steadily away from the ship, quickly disappearing from sight among the fringing trees. She was about to give vent to her surprise when she heard, up above, the whispering thunder of another ship. He had his head back, too.

"That is more like what I had figured," he murmured. "High-jackers! Third party steps in to scoop the pool. Don't move just yet, ma'am. Let's see what this lot do."

It was an entirely different kind of ship. That was apparent by the stronger note of the jets as it rode down, and was also obvious to the eye. She stared up in astonishment, and then looked at Joe, but he had his head down on his chest and his eyes closed. Some intuition made her keep silent until he raised his head and looked at her bleakly.

"This one is the trouble," he said softly. "That first pair were full of fun—the jokers. But this lot—they aren't playing patty-cake!" He showed his teeth in what she was coming to realize was his anger response. "Feels like two people, not friendly at all!"

The last word was the key that fitted everything into place in her mind, confirmed as she stared at him and saw the bright blue flower head poking out from his hair and aiming at the ship.

"Look here," she demanded, the words refusing to be stopped now. "Just how far can that flower thing reach anyway? And what does it do, whisper in your ear?"

Disconcertingly, she now saw him smile in real amusement, a grin that wiped ten years off his age in as many seconds. "You catch on fast. Took me a long while to find out just what Friendly could do. I wouldn't be hard and fast about range. It depends a lot on the quality and intensity of the emotion, I reckon. And I don't know how, either—not in technical terms. Just educated guessing is all. I told you about the plants being sensitive to emotional fields, didn't I? Well, Friendly, here, goes a step better than that. He acts like a kind of transducer-amplifier. He detects 'em, and I feel 'em through him, like a kind of antenna. There's a bit more to it than that, but that's enough—"

He fell silent. Shock waves began to smash to and fro between the forest and the mountains at their back.

"Sounds like a Navy craft," he said, pitching his voice over the din. "Better watch this, it feels pretty bad!"

She cupped her hands over her ears and watched the squat black bulk of the ship hammer down over its own jet-braking. She could identify the profile now; a medium-range Fleet Scout with the marking erased.

"A pirate!" she shouted in amazement.

"Couldn't be anything else," he snapped back. "That's no service crew aboard there. See what he's doing?"

She saw, and at first she didn't believe it and wanted to think that it was a trick of vision or an accident. It was no accident that kept the spouting fire-tail aimed directly at the slim, helpless ship that stood there. Down and down, under the ruthless hand of a competent pilot, the scout pitched and swayed but never lost aim. The seething cascade of blue-white fire swept down and licked and blotted out Delmar's ship altogether—and held there remorselessly, while Selena let out an anguished breath in a soundless cry of protest. Then, with renewed fury, the black ship lifted up and away, to come down efficiently about fifteen yards clear. Again the echoes rushed in to fill an aching silence, and she stared at the warped and sagging, molten caricature of what had been an elegant space-coupe.

"Like I said"—Joe's matter of fact drawl was jarring in the quiet—"not the friendly type. I wonder where in time they learned *that* stunt?"

"Who . . ." It came out a squeak, and she tried again. "Who would do a thing like that? And why?" Anger hadn't come yet. She was still getting over the stunned shock of seeing a ship destroyed.

"Looks like somebody didn't want your friends to leave."

"If that's all it was. Suppose they had still been in there?"

"They must've been seen to get out. Let's hope so, anyway. Thing is, what do we do now?"

"We must do something." She was urgent about that. "We can't just—"

"Just what? Whoever's in that ex-Navy ship is liable to take a poor view of anything we do in the way of interference."

"You're being a coward again."

"No, ma'am, just careful. We still don't know a great deal about what's going on. We could find out a bit more."

"How?"

"You ever climbed a tree?"

"I have. I might not be as good at it as you are, but I'll manage."

"That's fine. Let's go." He ducked out of their shallow refuge and around the crest of rock until they were out of view from the plain. Then he halted her with a sharp stare from his bright eyes. "Get one thing, though. We're going to snoop—to lie low and listen—maybe learn a thing or two. That's all. Don't go horning in with that weapon of yours. Remember there's at least four of them, maybe more, and there's only two of us."

"You don't have to spell it out."

"Just so long as we know how it is. Come on." He went away down the rugged rock slope like a sleek cat. She plunged after him, and it took her only seconds to realize that he had been holding himself back previously. Now he seemed to be in a hurry, and no matter how she slid and scrambled she was far behind him when he achieved level and plunged into the first of the undergrowth. By the time she reached it he was nowhere to be seen or heard, and she plowed to a standstill, feeling lost and terrified in a way she hadn't known since childhood. Panic fed on itself, and, too late, she felt the touch and clutch of snaking twigs, of eager branches and prickling thorns insinuating themselves in and around her chain-mail dress and pressing hungrily close to her skin. She tried to duck, to dodge, but that was worse than useless, and within gasping seconds she was caught fast. It was all she could do to make herself be still, shivering. And there he was, showing his teeth and sneering at her.

"What are you throwing a panic for? You *want* these plants to eat you?"

"I was lost—I didn't know where you'd gone!"

"Take a breath. Be glad to see me, even if you aren't. Work on that. I thought I told you there was nothing could hurt you here so long as you're friendly? Don't you believe that?"

"I can't help it," she snapped, as the clutching strands refused to let go. "I'm no wood nymph. I was brought up civilized."

"That's nice. You'll die civilized too unless I can do something to stop it. We haven't a lot of time, so you'll have to excuse me. Maybe this'll help you out." He came close, put out his hand and touched her at the joint of neck and shoulder. His fingers were firm and strong, yet cool—and she was hard put to resent his touch, although she wanted to—but then something else came. All at once the entire scene was subtly different. She heard all of it thinking. It was not in words, not in any way she could translate; it was just an awareness of life like the instruments of some muted but mighty orchestra. Sighing trees breathed huge sleepy organ tones; grass rippled a constant piccolo chatter; the clutching bushes scolding and suspicious, yelped, aggressively angry at being disturbed and upset. She gasped at the revelation and denial rose into her mind instantly.

I didn't mean to hurt you, to intrude. Truly! I didn't know. I really am sorry. This is your home, and I'm blundering in. The thoughts modulated as she felt the hostility ebbing away. The binding strands loosened, curled away, withdrew, and the bad-tempered yelping abated to a murmur. Then he took his hand away and it was all gone, like switching off a radio.

"I'd no idea," she breathed. "Not that it was—like that! They're just like people!"

SIX

"DON'T BEAR down too hard on that," he warned. "Friendly is inclined to exaggerate a little. They do have personality, though."

"Is it like that for you all the time?"

For the first time, she saw him discomfited a little. "That's a big question, and we don't have gabbing time, right now. We need a tree."

He led once more and she had a gritty moment of irritation in thinking that she seemed to have done nothing these past hours, except trail at his heels. But that went rapidly as she struggled to keep up to him in the winding wilderness all about them. Perhaps that momentary contact with the sensitive plant had cracked some unguessed barrier in her mind, for it now seemed that the wild luxuriance of bushes, creepers and great standing trees was a kindly and welcoming place. Perhaps it was imagination, but it no longer seemed as if she had to push through or watch her feet for tripping roots—as if the wildlife was edging aside to let her through. He stopped again.

"This will do us."

She stared indignantly up into the spread of a forest giant, the trunk of which was at least five feet through. "The nearest branch is all of nine feet up," she pointed out. "What do we do, fly?"

"Hold that!" He thrust the spear at her, and proceeded to walk up the knotty trunk on his fingers and toes. It was impossible, but she watched him do it as if he had hooks on his fingertips and toes. She breathed hard. Selena Ash was long accustomed to commanding admiration and awe, to being in front of the competition and to affecting disdain for compliments because she knew she had earned them. It was not so here.

"If you expect me to do that . . ."

"The spear," he called. "Grab the pointed end and hold on; pass the other end up here."

She did that. He stooped, took hold, and she was swept into the air like a feather, until her feet could kick out and find rest on the branch.

"I reckon you can manage the rest." He set the spear aside in a fork and scrambled around and up. She breathed hard again, then followed. "We have a little while," he called down to her from above. "Your friends are getting close. But we have a while."

A thousand questions choked her mind as she climbed. One question in particular bothered her: If he could sense and evaluate people at such great distances, by means of that plant, why was it that she had felt absolutely nothing of him when he had touched her? Did he know what she was thinking and feeling? If so, he didn't seem to care much. But now, with a heave and kick, she was around to where she could see her own ship, and hear thrashing sounds at a distance to tell her that someone was not far away. She hauled herself on to a branch close to him, blowing hard.

"I wonder you don't just take off and hurl yourself from branch to branch. Wouldn't that be quicker for you?" she muttered.

"Brachiation," he murmured, and the word came oddly in his hillbilly drawl. "That's for fiction. You ever see a competition athlete? Those laddies who do stunts on the rings and bars? Even the best of them couldn't swing far hand to hand. Can't be done. The human frame isn't built for it. And getting mad about things don't change them any. 'Comes your friends, now."

The ship was so close she could have hit it with a thrown stone. She lay along her branch and turned her head in the direction of the coming noise. Voices became intelligible.

"Can you see the ship yet, Robin?"

"I see it. And about time! What the hell was she thinking of, to sit down in this damned jungle?" Robin Delmar staggered into view through the bushes, and Selena caught her breath. He was tall, black-haired and bronzed as an Amerind, with his head high and that sardonic, crooked grin on his lean face; it was the triumph of poise over reality. He was a mess. The dark close-fitting tunic with the up-and-down stripe that he favored because it made him look even more angular and lean than he was was a ruin, hanging in torn and molten shreds from shoulders and waist. His bared skin was streaked with green and scarred with angry red scratches and patches. As he halted, she saw that his belt, boots, and the strap that held his tracking instrument were whole—and that he shook, visibly, either from strain or shock.

In a moment she saw Pierre Lacoste coming after and he was worse. He looked scared out of his mind, his butter-blond hair dangling in his eyes and his jaw slack, no sign remaining of his boyish Gallic charm. He, too, had been clawed by the plants, and both men were gleaming with sweat.

"Go on," Lacoste cried. "What are we waiting for? Let's get aboard and away from here."

"Me, too," Delmar declared. "Only, how? No gangway out."

Lacoste ran unsteadily, to where the exit hatch stood shut, and stared at it. "Selena," he screamed. "Open up. For

God's sake, let us in!" He drew breath for another scream and reeled as Delmar hit him.

"Button it, Pierre. Just button it, see? You want to point the whole world right at us? If she's in there, she knows we're here. No need to scream your stupid head off!"

"They're so scared," Selena murmured aside to Joe, "it's a wonder they got this far through the bushes."

"Scared of whoever might be chasing 'em. I doubt they so much as noticed the plants—so they wouldn't attack all that hard. Just get a little stirred up, is all."

"What do you mean, if she's in there?" Lacoste demanded, from his knees. "Where else would she be? She's got to be in there, if she's alive."

"Cut that talk! Why wouldn't she be alive?"

"Why is she here, anyway? You told me—you *told* me— the ship was fixed to warp out in space—"

"That's right. And I disconnected her courser so she couldn't move anywhere else; and we were waiting for her. We saw her warp out. So?" Delmar sounded as if his patience had worn thin; Lacoste had lost his altogether.

"So?" he shrilled. "If you fixed it so damned clever, why is the ship here, and not there!" Under stress his French origins began to show.

"Because," Delmar growled, "our Selena is just that much smarter than we figured. I *told* you the whole scheme was a damned juvenile notion. All I did was disconnect six or seven relays. She could be just smart enough to unfix those."

"But what is she doing here?"

"Having a big laugh at us, I reckon. She's earned it."

"But our ship? And that other ship?" Lacoste was shaking, pleading. Selena felt ashamed for him. "We could have been all burned up!"

"Cool it." Delmar sneered. "That was a Navy craft. You know who her old man is; you know the kind of strings she could pull—and you know how she can spit when she has a mind."

"I don't believe it. She wouldn't do anything like that!"

"You have a better answer?" Delmar swung away from his companion, raised his gaze to the camera immediately above the exit hatch, and made a parody of a bow to it.

"I hereby pronounce *uncle* for both of us, my dear Selena," he said, "but don't linger too long to gloat, sweetheart.

There could be several unkind characters on our tail right now. We'd like in!"

Selena stirred, and Joe hissed an instant warning.

"Now look," she muttered. "This has gone far enough. Those boys are in bad trouble."

"Trouble is right. Worse than you think, and headed right this way. Coming fast. We're safer on the outside."

She hesitated, and then it was too late.

"Turn around. Make it slow." The grating voice was harshly thick with authority. Both men swung much too fast, but froze as they stared into a magnum-beamer, steady as death in the hand of the man who held it. "Well, well," he growled. "Hot-Shot Delmar and Lover-Boy Lacoste. Where's the dame?"

"Who the hell are you?" Delmar challenged, then staggered back as the turf at his toes poofed into smoke and stink.

"I'm asking the questions, mister. If it matters, I'm Pardoe. Bernard Pardoe. And this"—he jerked his head slightly to his rear—"is Miss Scorpia Martine. You know who you are. Now, where's the dame? I mean, Miss Selena Ash, no less."

"We don't know!" Lacoste found his tongue. "We haven't seen her. We suppose she's still in there."

Pardoe grinned. "You suppose, huh? Maybe we can sharpen that up a bit. Scorpia, take a gentle stroll around and see if she's hid out somewhere close by. Don't take any chances now."

"Who, me?" Miss Martine smiled. Watching them, Selena had wondered how they had come so far through the same undergrowth that had savaged Delmar and Lacoste without being affected at all, now she knew. Miss Martine had a magnum-beamer of her own set now to broad beam and low power. She used it lavishly to scorch a way through any bushes that stood in her path. And she was efficient, too. Selena watched her and felt resentful, for a moment, that any woman should be so flawlessly beautiful, so outrageously shaped.

She shifted her stare to Pardoe, remembering him from the spy record but realizing now that this solid slab of a man was even uglier than his picture. His cold black eyes never once left his two captives until Miss Martine had thoroughly covered the perimeter of the ship.

"All clean, Buck. No sign. Reckon she is inside?"

"She's no fool." Pardoe frowned horribly. "Going to take some hooking out of there."

"Stand-off!" Delmar taunted, and Pardoe glared at him. "You talk too much, Hot-Shot. Just try remembering that I don't need you all that much."

"All right." Delmar shrugged wearily. "Just what do you need, if not us? What are you doing here anyway, apart from destroying my ship?"

Pardoe hunched over his weapon, then slowly relaxed. "No," he muttered, arguing with himself. "Let's not discard something we might be able to play. You crumbs are friends of hers. If she *is* in there, getting an eyeful and listening, maybe she'll think again if she sees her friends getting fried, nice and slow. What d'you reckon, Scorpia?"

"I'd like that. Especially him, he's so tough!" Miss Martine showed her teeth and moved back to be out of range of the smell she anticipated. Pardoe smiled.

"I don't know what happened to your drapes, Hot-Shot, but it saves a minute, doesn't it? And this is gonna hurt you more'n it does me—"

Miss Martine stepped back just a bit too far. Selena saw, from a different viewpoint, what she had experienced only a few hours earlier. Two luxuriant head-high bushes leaned together in unison and flung their snaking branches eagerly around Miss Martine's neck, waist, arms, and legs. She screeched once, and went over backwards, struggling wildly; relays of twigs and branches folded over to grab at her. Pardoe froze with his chin on his shoulder.

"What the hell are you doing?"

"Get—me—out—of this!" The confused mass of greenery thrashed wildly; Miss Martine screeched again. "Help! I'm being eaten!"

Pardoe whirled, took half a dozen heavy steps, crouched to stare and then used his beamer on the wrist-thick stem of one bush, slicing it apart in a spurt of green smoke. Then the snakelike coils were still. He plucked and pulled, flinging the leafy things away as he coughed at the stench and fumes. Delmar saw what he thought was a chance and launched himself at Pardoe's back. The big man reacted like lightning, spinning, straightening up and swinging his hand around with the beamer in it. It struck Delmar's head. Pardoe glared at Lacoste.

"You care to try something like that, Lover-Boy?" Lacoste cringed and Pardoe turned his head. "Scorpia, you all right? What the hell happened?"

"I don't believe it!" She was shrill with indignant astonishment as she struggled to her feet and threw away the last dead coils of bush and twig. "Those damned shrubs went for me. They're alive!"

"Of course they're alive."

"That's not what I mean, dammit! They grabbed me! I tell you, they were dragging me down and starting to eat me. Just take a look at my duds!"

Pardoe looked, and made what was probably his idea of a laugh. "I would never have believed plants had them kind of ideas. They got you down to the buff, nearly."

"They got further than that!" she dabbed at herself and winced. "Hey, maybe this stuff is poisonous."

"Forget it. Those two are still breathing, aren't they? At least—take a look at Delmar, will you? Maybe I hit him too hard."

"The hell with him! What about me? You expect me to stroll around this damned jungle in the raw?"

"You'll crawl on your knees if I say so, and like it. Take a look at him and let me think."

SEVEN

UNWILLINGLY, trying to rescue the shreds of her clothing, Miss Martine went to kneel by Delmar and investigate his condition—none too gently. Pardoe turned to the silent ship; he scowled at it.

"I'm going to toast your friends, Miss Ash. It will be interesting to see how much of it you can stand." He turned again and aimed his weapon at Lacoste. Selena stirred.

"I can't take any more of this."

"You hold still," Joe muttered. "He's only bluffing. He can't scare that feller any more than he's scared right now, and he knows it."

The beamer held steady. Lacoste shut his eyes in terror. Pardoe snarled and lowered the weapon.

"Bitch!" he growled. Miss Martine glanced at him from her crouch.

"She's no fool, Buck. Why would she come out? What's to gain?"

"Yes. How's the tough guy?"

"He'll live." She got to her feet again, and with an angry vehemence, dragged at the last shreds of her clothes and flung them away. She began patting and rubbing herself in a vain attempt to get ease. "Look, think of something, will you? And fast—I'm going crazy with this itch!"

Pardoe turned once more to stare at the ship. Frustration was obvious in every line of his bulky body.

"I play you one more game," he growled, and strode to where one landing foot had settled into the turf. It was a pointless sign of his need to get close, to get violent. He glared up.

"I know you're in there!" he roared. "Smart, huh? Well, you just listen to me. You better come out, and soon!" He swung his free hand into a fist and slammed it against the metal. Selena winced, knowing what was coming next. The high-frequency twister field that lurked invisibly in the metal wrenched Pardoe's arm away, spun him completely around and sent him careening away in knotted convulsions. The beamer fell from his twitching hand. Before he could regain control he had plunged headlong into a thicket nearby. Once again the eager bushes closed in, smothering, binding, gouging, constricting and biting. This time it was Miss Martine's turn to stand and stare open-mouthed, and then to hoist her beamer and run.

Then she halted, frantically trying to weigh the situation. This time it wasn't so easy to spot the main stems. She adjusted to needle-beam and sliced away at one side, right down to the soil. Coughing as the acrid fumes rolled out, she swung and sliced at the other side. Selena could hardly see her for the smoke; but her voice was audible.

"Hold still, Buck. I can't get at the roots at all. I'm setting for wide on low and I'll toast them off you. Hold still, now!"

Out of the roiling smoke came muted sizzlings, then yells from Pardoe as the temperature rose. In a moment, Miss

Martine came backing out to whip round and flourish the weapon at Lacoste. There was no threat, and she relaxed, backing away to let Pardoe come staggering out of the smoke. He slapped at singed twigs and cursed fervently. Bits of his tailored black tunic came away. He was more gross uncovered, and his body was coming up in red weals. Miss Martine did not stare at him, nor did she make any comment about his condition.

"Let's get out of here, Buck, huh? What say we just fry this pair and blow? I've had just about all I can take of these damned educated plants!"

"Hah!" He shivered, then stared at her strangely. "What did you call them?"

"You ought to know by now. They grabbed you, didn't they? And didn't they play possum until you were close enough to grab? What else would you call them?"

"Yes. That's what I was thinking, too. Come over here a minute."

The pair moved away to be out of earshot of their captives, and, unwittingly, directly under the tree where Selena and Joe were hidden.

"What's on your mind, Buck?"

"This place. Add it up, Scorpia—an uncharted system, right off the charts and—your words—educated plants. What else could it be?"

"If you're thinking what I think you're thinking—nuts! Look, we listened in on those crumbs, didn't we? Delmar deliberately picked his spot to be far away, but random. And neither of those dims knew a thing about this place before they landed here, that's sticking out a mile."

"So all right, they drew it out of a hat. I'm not saying different. I'm saying that this is it."

"You mean, by accident?"

"Why not? Look, Columbus went looking for China, and see where he ended up. Stranger things have happened. Unless there are two planets like this, which I don't believe."

"All right." She shrugged, scratching herself. "What's the play?"

"It wants figuring to do it right."

"Why don't we just fade, let them get together and blow and then take possession?"

"Use your head. If we let them get away, they'll be

back with half the damned fleet, busting to take us apart. Remember who the Ash dame is, will you? Besides, those three aren't all that dumb—especially her. Give them a chance to think it through and they'll get it, just like you did. And everybody has heard of Jensen's Planet, even if they don't believe it."

"All right," she repeated impatiently. "So what do we do?"

"I think I know. Somehow, we have to keep 'em all here until I have checked out and made sure this is the place I think it is. After that, we'll see. But first I have to fix this Ash dame. I think I'm wise to her."

The pair turned and marched back to where Lacoste was kneeling and Delmar had raised himself on an elbow, blood staining the side of his face.

"Beauty and the Beast," he said, and Pardoe grunted.

"You don't learn, do you, comic? Pay attention, both of you. When you two comedians worked out your little scheme to play a trick on Miss Ash, you picked your coordinates at random, right? Want to qualify that, now?"

"You seem to know all about it already," Delmar retorted.

"Most of it. That's my business, and I'm good at it. Me and Scorpia, here, we study folk like you for pickings. Either one of you would be worth about half a million stellars to your friends. But then there was Miss Ash too, and she's worth a bit more than that, quite a bit. So, when you handed us the chance to knock off all three of you at once, naturally we were delighted to play along. You picked this area at random?"

"I had nothing to do with that." Lacoste spoke quaveringly. "The idea, it was mine, but Robin worked out the details."

"Not at random," Delmar said. "You think I'm a fool? I picked a spot that was far away from everything—off the charts and main trade routes. So what? I'd like to know how you got on to it. You never bugged us on that detail."

"Tricks in all trades—and we all have questions. I would love to know how this ship got from there to here. When we followed you aboard and checked over what you had fixed—and made a note of the courser settings—I wired in a destruct module, all set to blow the guts out of her as

44

soon as she warped out. You could've thought of that, Hot-Shot!"

"A destruct in the courser?" Delmar sat up, got all the way to his feet and stood, swaying. "You fat slab of filth!"

"Watch the big words, crumb, or I'll straighten out your head. You will kindly notice that it didn't happen. She not only located your monkeyshines and fixed them, she also fixed my little blessing. And, I can tell you, I had three tracers stuck on her hull, just in case yours folded. She had scratched yours and two of mine. And mine were boobied with detonite. You chew on that a while, Delmar, and see what it adds up to. You were trying to get a rise out of her? Man, she's been playing you and just about everybody else."

He turned to face the ship again. "You better pay attention, Miss Ash. You're all through with the popsy playgirl bit, so forget it. And you are, like it or not, right up to here in something bigger than you may realize. You will have heard I'm sure, of a man called Jory Jensen?"

"Jory Jensen?" Delmar echoed, and even Lacoste showed interest.

"What is this all about now, Robin?"

"Search me. Pardoe, you're talking about that crazy scout who went and lost himself in space about four years ago. A nut—what has he got to do with anything? Don't tell me *you* believe all those fantastic yarns?"

"I'm through telling you anything." Pardoe did not turn. "You better listen, Miss Ash, and think. I'll draw you a diagram. Me and Scorpia are going back to my ship. We're taking your playmates with us. You should have knocked off that third tracer, but you didn't. I have an ear on it. If it stops I'll be back here, with muscles, and you'll be sorry. If you try to lift off with it still there, I'll catch you before you can warp out, and you'll be even sorrier. Mine is an ex-Navy ship, and it can do nasty things to you. So take a hint. Just stay right here and do nothing. You try anything —anything at all—and this bright pair will fry, immediate— and I'll send the cooked remains to your old man, with full details."

He waited, but there was no sign. He shrugged, turned to his visible audience. "All right, you two, get moving. That way."

"Look, be your age," Delmar shouted. "How the devil can

we walk anywhere? We wouldn't get ten steps through those bushes."

"It's a point, Buck," Miss Martine declared. "One of us better go on in front and clear a path. You?"

"Why me?"

"Because I'm modest," she snapped. "Why should I do these two any favors? You go ahead; I'll follow."

The last Selena saw of the strange parade was Miss Martine's shapely rear disappearing through the screening undergrowth. She stirred, feeling stiff and old, then turned to meet Joe's bright stare.

"Can you tell if they are really going away, that it's not just a trick?"

"Up to a point, sure. They're going away so far. What have you in mind to do?"

"I want to get into my ship and do a thing or two."

"Like lifting off?"

"Don't be stupid! Pardoe meant what he said and you should know that with that ship of his he could blast me into scrap without trying. No, I just want to fix something. It won't take long."

"Still going away. You have time enough, I reckon." He squirmed and went down the tree as easily as a squirrel. He was standing under the tree long before she had reached the lowest branch. She slid down to her stomach, then painfully to arm's length and dangled.

"You'll have to help me, please."

He turned, touched her ankle and caught her as she let go. In that moment she had, again, that awesome sense of being surrounded by murmuring life, but it vanished as he put her down and stood away.

"Still going away," he said. "You'll have time."

"I don't want you to run off."

"You don't need me now. Nothing either of us can do anyway. Pardoe holds all the cards."

"I have no intention of sitting stupidly in my ship awaiting Mr. Pardoe's pleasure. A sitting duck?" He shrugged fractionally. "I'd rather hide out, and for that I need your help again."

"I have things to do for my own self, ma'am."

"Oh well, at least wait there until I come out again, and

we can talk about it a little. Will you? I'll be no more than ten minutes. You can keep watch."

He shrugged again. "All right, ma'am. Can't hurt."

EIGHT

THE MOST important thing she had to do didn't take her more than one tenth of her bargained-for time, which left her an interval in which to do a few other things. One was to study herself in a mirror much more critically than she had done in a long time. Then realizing that she was wasting time, she got out a long-range beamer rifle and a three-pack of spare charges, and her portable code sender, and went out.

He stood close to a tree, turning his head as she stepped clear of the gangway and whistled the notes that sealed her ship again. She searched around and found a hiding place for the small set—by the foot of the tree where he stood.

"That's it," she announced. "I'm in your hands now. How's the enemy, by the way?"

"Still going. That Pardoe's a bad man to play with," Joe said.

"I don't intend to play. I intend to let others do it for me. Joe, I've deceived you, just a little. I'm sorry. You didn't ask what it was I had to do, just now, in my ship. I'll tell you. Do you know what a Dirac-sender is?"

If she had kicked him in the stomach he couldn't have wilted more visibly. His face was gray under his tan as he muttered, "You can't mount a Dirac in a little hopper like that."

"Oh yes. It's a rather special ship."

"You don't have enough power!"

"I do—only just. It is set to repeat just one message, at fifteen minute intervals, and that, as you seem to know, eats up every erg the drive can store up. So, you see, I couldn't take off even if I wanted to, and I don't. You are surprisingly well-informed, Joe."

"For what good that is, now. You know what you've done?"

"I think so." She felt compunction at his obvious misery. "Joe—it was also right, what Pardoe said, about this planet, wasn't it?"

"You know it all, don't you? A damned Dirac! I told you"—he grew suddenly savage—"that I had things of my own to do. You have any idea what? You heard what Pardoe said. Do you have any notion what he's going to be doing, as soon as ever he can?" She felt his fury like a blast of heat, noting with an inconsequential part of her attention that he had forsaken his pose. "He'll break out a skimmer—a jet-copter—and he'll go looking for something. His proof, as he called it."

"Yes," she agreed. "I can understand that. He will go looking for a particular tree—Jory Jensen's miracle tree, on the planet of educated plants."

"The Tree," he groaned, his tone putting it into capitals.

"That's right, the Tree. But isn't that quite a task, finding one tree among millions? Or are there a lot of them?"

"Only the one that I know of. And he'll find it. Not right off, maybe, but he'll find it. I was meaning to get there first."

"To do what? Tangle with Pardoe? After warning me not to?"

"There's a difference. I live here; I know this place and the Tree; I know what it can *do*."

"And you know what Buck Pardoe can do, too. Joe, let me help."

"Help? What's the point, now you've alerted—whoever you're sending the Dirac for?"

"Let me worry about that when the time comes. Joe, don't be so damned stubborn. You can't go up against Pardoe on your own, with just a spear. And what about those two boys? All right, they got themselves into the mess, but they're friends of mine. They need help; and so do you. Go on, damn you, admit it! You've been independent so long you can't think any other way, that's your trouble."

He was racked with indecision, and she kept after him. "I have a beam rifle and I know how to use it. You know where the Tree is, and he doesn't. It's going to take him time to find it, which gives us an edge—and the chance to figure out some kind of strategy. Two heads are better than one. I was the unwitting cause of all this mess; let me help you."

He sighed and hunched his shoulders. "All right, ma'am, you sold me. Don't seem to have any choice, not now."

"Do me just one small favor, will you? Stop calling me ma'am. I am not ancient, academic or married. My name is Selena."

"Whatever you say. Can we go now?"

"I think so—hey, what about food? I've just realized I'm as empty as a drum."

"If you can hang on for maybe half an hour, that can be fixed. Let's go."

Here we go again, she mused, *him leading the way and me tagging along after.* As they plunged into the trackless riot of undergrowth, it seemed that the tangled bushes and creepers did tend to get out of the way—or was it just accumulating skill and experience? Either he was holding himself back on her account or she was getting good at moving through jungle, having little trouble keeping up with him. So many questions bubbled in her mind as they strode along that she ventured to put some of them into words.

"Of course they get out of our way," he said, with just a tint of surprise in his voice at her question. "Plants don't like being knocked and bruised and trampled on, any more than you do."

She demurred, "It's not as obvious as you make it sound. It wants a bit of getting used to, meeting plants that think and have emotions."

"They don't think," he corrected. "Not what we would call thinking. But they do have senses. Why shouldn't they? What's so surprising about that? Anything that lives has senses of some kind?"

"Senses?"

A faint but genuine smile plucked at the corner of his mouth. They moved on a while in silence. Then he veered aside and brought her to a small clearing by a tree and halted.

"Senses," he murmured. "You ever wondered why bushes don't grow under and around a tree?"

"Because they need sunshine, I suppose. That's not intelligent—just chemistry, isn't it?"

"It might be, only some bushes, and creepers do grow around the bases of trees—the parasitic kind. Chemistry? And what about grass, doesn't it need sunshine?" He had no need to point to the thick carpet of grass they stood on. She frowned. "Did you ever wonder why most trees have spaces around them, between them?"

"Look—I don't know. I'm no botanist. I imagine it's purely mechanical. Seeds, nuts, or whatever fall and try to take root, and can't unless there is room enough for them to grow properly. You tell me."

"It's better if you find out for yourself. Take a good look at any tree. Do you ever see the branches bumping into each other? Look at the leaves—all carefully separated. Or just look, really look, at a patch of grass—this grass. Come on." He squatted down and invited her to do the same. "A host of leaves, millions of them, all separate from each other —because this is something a plant has: a sense of space, it's own space. All plants have the ability to work out enough space for their needs. It's territorial awareness—just like birds or bees—or most animals. Or people, for that matter; only, with people it's so weak that they don't use it. They just feel neurotic and go mad when they are overcrowded."

She knelt, put one hand on his shoulder to steady herself, and moved instantly into that strange and fascinating dimension of awareness of the seething sentience all around. Little voices and shrill, big sighs and deep, restless gossiping, an ocean of minds—and she felt him start to lean away.

"Oh, please, no. Don't spoil it. Who'd ever believe that even the blades of grass talk to each other? It's so wonderful!"

"It's not talk," he corrected mildly. "Remember what I said about birds? And I suppose it is stretching a point to call it emotion. They have a way of knowing when they have enough room and when something is getting too close, which causes distress of some kind. I suppose maybe it is emotion, at that. We humans tend to make a lot out of very little, when you think of it. There are only two basic feelings about anything. Either it's favorable—for you—or it isn't. You like it, or you don't. Shade it whichever way you like, but it works out the same. Positive or negative. Every living thing has it. You know yourself, surely, that feeling of being close to something that disturbs you?"

"Yes. Yes, I do." She veered away from that quickly. "But what about the mobility?"

"That's something I don't know. Mobile plants aren't new.

Even on Earth you can find them: mimosa, fly-catchers. And all plants move, anyway, only very slowly. Maybe there's something in the soil or air here. But the sense of space is old. And that's what Friendly is good at, and what you're getting, through him."

"And much more," she declared. "Much more than just space—feelings, too. But why does it sound like music, almost?"

"I don't know that. Why does some music make you feel good, or happy, or like dancing, or sad? I suppose plants just feel good when they have all the room they need, and upset when anything threatens that. And so they can respond to anything else that happens to feel something, like an echo. But that's just a guess." He stood up slowly, and she arose with him, keeping her hand on his shoulder; she was reluctant to lose contact.

"I hate to part with all this," she confessed, "but I can't very well keep my hand on your shoulder all the time. Couldn't I hold your hand?"

That invisible curtain slid down over his face. "That might not be such a bright idea," he declared. "Not right away."

"Whatever do you mean? Are you afraid that I would be intruding on your space, or something?" She snatched away her hand, and the unseen orchestra winked out of her mind. "If you object to me touching you, just say so."

"That's one of the reasons," he said, baring his teeth in that biting smile. "You tend to get spitty real easy— the least little thing—and I can feel it bad enough at a distance, without getting it full blast firsthand."

"Oh!" She snatched a hand to her face, felt the hot blood of chagrin burning there and then all over her body as mingled shame, and rage and humiliation shook her. "Did you have to be so brutally frank about it?"

"And that's another thing. Plants don't have a lot of crazy mixed up feelings. They don't try to hide anything or fake anything. You know exactly what the score is, with them."

"I see. And you're not capable of dealing with anything more complex than a vegetable, is that it?"

"Now you're real scratchy. And all knotted up, too. Your words say one thing, your voice says something else and Friendly tells me something altogether different from either. I let you hold my hand, you're going to get *me* all tangled up, too, and I just don't have time for that. We have quite a way to go yet."

Suddenly it struck her that he was speaking nothing but the plain truth, that she was mixed up, inside—and that he must have been getting the full blast of that, raw and un-diluted, every time he touched her. That idea ran to its logical conclusion and she flamed hotter than before. He must have sensed her feelings, *all* her feelings. She turned away helplessly, wishing herself a million miles away.

"No need to feel so bad about it, ma'am," he mumbled. "Can we get on now? Be time to eat in a while. It's not far."

"You go on ahead," she said, drilling herself to be calm. "I'll try not to offend you too much."

He hunched his shoulders in resignation and led off.

NINE

As THE best way to banish her shameful display from mind, Selena started paying extra attenton to the surroundings, trying to get some idea of the variation in species and ap-pearance of the various plants. She wondered about wild-life that ran. Surely, too, there had to be insects where there were flowers? Otherwise, what about pollination? It seemed a safe topic to be curious about, and she asked him as they moved along.

"Never seen any insects," he admitted, "big or small. Never thought much about it. I suppose they wouldn't have much chance with flowers like we have here—probably never got started. As for pollination, that's not always necessary. What is important, more, is the ability to disperse seeds and these bushes have all sorts of ways of doing that."

He showed her a few, indicating them as they came up on their way. She saw one gorgeous bush that threw para-chutes into the air, another that exerted pressure on its ber-ries until they popped out and one, with a particularly red bloom, that he warned her against.

"Not now—it's in flower. But around seed time, that's a good one to keep away from. The seeds form in a long row along a flexible spine, all sticking out like the teeth on a comb. And as they mature, the spine gets bent more and more, until it rips loose at the thin end, and flips the seeds off like needles—in a shower. The least thing will set them off, and they travel anything up to thirty feet."

Now their way was uphill and the luxuriance began to thin a little. The undergrowth dwindled, and the trees were slighter and not so tall. Long open vistas between the trunks were more and more common, affording her occasional glimpses of the mountains ahead. They came to a larger stream, almost a torrent, and he halted, waiting for her.

"This next bit is going to be unpleasant," he warned, "and you might wonder why, so I'll tell you now. Saves argument. This water leads where we want to go, and you'd think we would travel along the bank, but we're going to wade *in* it, because there's a peculiar kind of amphibian to be found hereabouts, that lurks mostly close by the water. They're about three inches long, but with teeth like a crocodile. I call 'em crock-beetles, and they're the one thing Friendly can't pick up—can't, or won't. So we take no chances. You'll hear 'em; they click. But they move like slick lightning, too, and by the time you hear 'em they're going away again, with a piece of your toe. So—it will be chilly, but it's the best way. Right?"

"Whatever you say."

"All right, but remember, it's cold. And no point in stopping, once we start. Be about twenty minutes, at most. Here we go."

She watched him plunge in almost to his knees, and turn to go upstream, and she followed—and was hard put not to squeal at the icy bite of the water. She plunged on, gritting her teeth against the pain—and saw first one, then another and then scurrying swarms of the things they were avoiding. They did click, and when she saw what with, she was almost resigned to the bitter cold of the water. They were hideous things with eight scaly legs. They glittered in shades of blue and green like animated jewels—but she saw the jaws and set her teeth.

They fought their way around a slow arc and came to a shelving stretch of silver sand. He went ahead and out. She staggered after him on lifeless stumps, and caught her breath as the circulation started trickling back like liquid needles.

"It's rough," he said, sympathizing with her unspoken ache, "but you feel fine in a while. All right to drink, too, if you're dry?"

"My stomach will feel insulted, it's so vacant."

"That's all right." He waved an arm ahead. "Food and drink just in sight. Go ahead and drink, if you want to. Get a real appetite!"

"All right." She knelt carefully in the sand and laved her face with the chilly water, managed to swallow a mouthful or two of it, and it made her teeth ache. But it also made her feel ravenous and she followed eagerly to where he had settled under a broad-spreading tree.

"Call this my bed-and-breakfast tree," he told her, plucking away at what seemed to be a mass of gray wool. Looking up, she saw that the tree was laden with similar bundles, each about the size of a cushion. Kneeling beside him she saw that he was uncovering a solid kernel. It was a dark green thing with a skin like a watermelon and about the same size. Balancing it on his left palm, he chopped at one end with his knife and uptilted it quickly.

"Here, that's yours. I'll get another. Drink first, and I'll split it afterwards."

It was more than half full of a pinkish liquid the texture of thin cream, but which tasted acid-sweet.

"It's certainly taken the edge off my appetite," she said, and he grinned up from carving one for himself.

"Filling, that stuff. I reckon you'd get fat as a pig if you lived here very long."

He got to work with his knife again, splitting the husk into three for her.

She munched heartily, enjoying the flavor and watched him with all her bottled-up curiosity returning. Yet she was reluctant to ask him personal questions in case she said anything to shatter this easy companionship that was so pleasant. He was neat in his movements and totally without self-consciousness; he was as natural as a wild animal and yet he was a man, and a cultured man, too, when he could be persuaded to stop acting innocent.

"I just don't understand you," she admitted at last, putting aside the last gnawed section of husk. "You seem to belong here so completely, and yet just four years ago you were an ordinary civilized human, like anyone else. Not that I'm blowing any trumpet for civilization," she added hastily as he got a bad-taste look on his face. "Right now I would have a hard job choosing between civilized luxury, and this. But that's an argument for some other time. What I mean," and she stretched and settled herself in comfort, using the discarded woolly fiber of the fruit as a kind of pillow, "is the way you have learned so much, so well. I count myself pretty resourceful; I've been trained to be. But I wouldn't care to take on this planet from scratch. I'd have been in a mess had it not been for you. And you had no one to help."

"I had the Tree," he said quietly.

"Is this it?" she queried, frowning up at the green spread and the gray-white hangings.

"No, not at all. You don't know so very much about the Tree, after all, or you wouldn't ask. But this one is pretty important, in its way. I'll show you, in a minute. First I have to tend to Friendly. He needs a drink, and he likes this stuff, too."

He went down to the river's edge and was back in a very short while, stuffing shredded bits of the fruit-meat into the pouch where the little plant had its roots.

"I said I had help from the Tree—the famous tree. But I also had a lot of help from Friendly, here. As I said before, it's more than just a sense of space and a sensitivity to emotions. I'm pretty sure he's learned something from me, and I sure have learned a lot from him. Like for instance." He reached out and took up the fleecy mass of stuff he had picked away from his own meal. "Watch this," he said, beginning to tug at the mass with careful fingers. In a moment she saw that he was unwinding it in a broad strip about nine inches almost like sheer linen. A silly question came to her mind.

"It just struck me—doesn't the tree mind when you pick its fruit?"

"No, why should it? The fruit, the seed, the spore, even the embryo within the mammalian body—is a separate entity. As soon as it's ready for a life of its own, it's discarded by the parent, isn't it? So why should the tree mind? Now this"—he had what looked like yards of the stuff by now—"is worth studying. It's light and fluffy so that it will catch any small breeze and be carried away. Or, if it falls into the water, and this kind of tree prefers to be near water, it will float and be carried away. And it's sensitive to temperature. Call that a chemical effect, if you like, but if I let go of it, it will roll itself up into a ball until it reaches a certain heat, on the inside. Then it will maintain it."

"That's something like incubation."

"That's right. Keeps the fruit at the right temperature for full growth, until it is ready to burst. But it's more than that, if you think a moment."

"You tell me," she prompted, feeling full and lazy. "I can't think around the corners the way you do."

"Well, it's close on sundown, and I need to sleep, so I guess you do, too. This is as good a place as any, right here. And this is your blanket. You just wrap it around yourself loosely, and it will do the rest. And there is more to it than that, even. We'll move as soon as it's light enough to see. And we will be heading up into the mountains. Not right to the top; I know a pass. But it will be pretty chilly up there."

"I see! But won't it be awkward, just wrapped around? Won't it keep coming undone all the time?"

"A few thorn hooks will fix that, and then you'll be fixed for the cold. Better than shivering in the thin stuff you're wearing now."

"Yes, of course. Thank you."

"Better get some sleep, now."

"Just like that? Both of us at once?"

"No danger, not here. In any case Friendly will warn me if anything does come up. Good night, ma'am."

As abruptly as that he stretched out, rolled over once or twice in the spread out fleece, wriggled and was still. She shook her head in quiet astonishment, spread and patted her own bundle until it was right, wriggled it around herself, and settled down. But there was far too much bubbling in her mind to let sleep come easily. The light faded rapidly, smudging everything into a purple blur; and then there was murmuring darkness. How pleasant it was! If only one could live like this, with no cares or worries, no duties or responsibilities—and no thought of the danger that was so close, postponed only for a brief while.

She let her mind drift back to the life that had been hers

only a short while ago, and the very memory of it was a bad taste. The remark of a colleague came back to her—a remark made in the shaking aftermath of a nearly fatal brush with certain citizens who objected to the law: "Just who are we busting a gut for—people? Are people really any better off now than they were in Cro-Magnon times? The good life! When you come right down to it, all the good life does for most people is make them fat, lazy and discontented."

That was an extreme, of course, but there was a lot of truth in it. She had never bothered to work out whether she was happy or not. She had been busy chasing the next thrill, the next sensation. Lying in the dark and thinking it over, she knew she had never been happy—not ever as blissfully contented as she was at the moment.

Then that thought went away. Pierre and Robin weren't having it as good as this, that was certain. She did have a job, duties, obligations. She hadn't dreamed it was going to be like this when she was assigned to find a planet. Memory played back to her a recording of her briefing interview.

"It's a bad one, Miss Ash." Admiral Longstaffe had been curt, possibly a bit upset by the peculiar turn of events that had put his employer's daughter in the chair opposite him. Longstaffe, thick-necked, red-faced and hard to please, was the presiding brain of Conway Ash Security, and he had every right to be hard to please. With disasters of the past still recent enough to chill the memory and not yet defeated, no new technological effort could be passed until it had been scrutinized down to the last atom, and that called for security of an order that permitted nothing less than one hundred percent. It also empowered Longstaffe to call in the help of a quasi-mythical organization known simply as the Philosophy Corps, when he found himself chewing on something big but outside his immediate competence. It must have shaken him considerably to have the fast reply from P.C. headquarters that his employer's daughter was the nearest and handiest agent they could supply. "You've had time to study the dossier?"

"Fully, what there is of it. Jory Jensen, space scout. Eccentric—what scout isn't? A man would have to be bent upstairs in some way, to take on the job in the first place. Brilliant, or he wouldn't qualify. So, a mad genius lost him-

self in space, somewhere in the general area of Epsilon
Aurigae about five years ago. The details about him are
trimmings, but give no hint why you want him found. Why?"

"We don't. You won't find him. He's dead."

TEN

SHE JABBED at the dossier with a finger, then sat back.
"Dead, eh? Why isn't it mentioned there? And what's the
point in my reading it?"

"Last first. You need all the information you can get, because we have so little. And his file is not closed simply
because—well, there's a lot more that could come."

"You are sure he's dead? You want his remains traced
and located, brought back, is that it?"

"Nothing like that. He lost himself on purpose because
he knew he was dying. A damned foolish thing to do, but if
a man can't choose what he wants to do with his last moments it's a poor world." Longstaffe coughed gruffly to cover
his sentimental lapse, and looked like going on.

"Just a minute. Dying?"

"Definitely. He went through the regulation physical and
mental check as soon as he reported from his last mission.
The signs indicated that he had at some time suffered a
bad exposure to mu-radiation. An accident with his warp
generator. He wasn't told that, mark you—just handed a
blue card and told to come back for a second check. That
is routine; it means hang on a bit, the machines have
found something wrong and we're checking. And that is true,
too. You don't jump to conclusions on a matter like that.
But he did; he knew. He left the reception complex and
went straight back to his ship and took off. That is the last
anyone has seen of him—or ever will, in all probability.
Prognosis four months, give or take a few days—and that's
over four years ago."

"Seems conclusive. But where do I come in?"

"Forget Jensen; let him lie, wherever he is. What we're
after is something he found and did not report. On the
way back from wherever, he stopped off for a bender on

Tau Ceti III—place they call Shangri-La. I imagine you know about it? Right, well, it's an old story. He fell in with a gang of sharpies. They got him stoned out of his mind, rolled him clean and left him to wake up with a hangover and regrets. So far as is known he came straight home from there—and the rest happened the way I've told you. He made no report at all, either there or at base, about the crooks. You can't figure a man like that."

"How do you know about it?"

"The same bunch got hooked by the Shangri-La law, a couple of days later, trying to clip and clean a tourist who happened to be a somebody and screamed. They were rounded up, and when the pressure went on them, they cracked. The point is that among the loot found in their possession was stuff identifiable as the property of Jory Jensen. A part of it was some sort of seeds. They claimed that Jensen had said those seeds were worth anything you cared to ask—a fortune. Shangri-La shipped the whole bundle to us, story and all—his chrono, pocketbook, lucky charm, solidos of half a dozen girl friends—the usual stuff—and the seeds. Of course, Jensen himself was gone by the time the package landed."

Longstaffe paused. "Miss Ash—we planted some of those seeds—the research department, that is. The results are pushing our best botanical research people—and others—into a slow mumble. They are so far from finding explanations that they are having trouble just believing their own results. Miss Ash, we have to know where that tree is."

"What were their findings?"

Longstaffe coughed again and looked portentous. "This is top security, remember—but what would you say to a plant or tree, that grows whatever you want? They selected ten of those seeds and each lab grew one. They were separate. One says, 'This looks very like a kind of citrus plant to me.' That specimen produced oranges—and lemons. Says another, 'I've seen something like this. I will bet it is related to cinchona.' He got what he was looking for. Then they started comparing notes—and with others. Flowers, creepers, other fruits, smells—you name it, or just imagine it—and the seeds deliver. The last reports I had was that the botanists were recruiting from chemists and physicists for complicated and tricky molecules to dream up, and getting them. They did not dare to bring their separate experiments together—for just one thing, if those damned plants can read a human mind, they can certainly read each others'—and you think about it for a while and you'll go lightheaded, too. We need that tree!"

She took a careful breath and objected. "But if Jensen is dead, as you say, and made no report on whatever the planet was where he got those seeds—four years ago—how can it be found?"

"I know; it's hopeless. We have every unit we can spare out looking as diligently as possible without stirring up curiosity among others. A needle in the biggest damned haystack anyone ever thought of. But Jensen talked once, that much we know; he may have talked to other people. Somebody might have seen something, heard something, probably without realizing it was anything important. You'll start from Shangri-La. You can pass yourself off as—yourself. And keep your ears and eyes open. If you get anything, anything at all—report. We, the forces of order and sanity, have to find that Anything Tree first!"

Selena could have given him a number of arguments about the forces of order and sanity, but she had to find the mysterious plant.

The forlorn impression that the search would be for nothing had grown swiftly as she listened to the fanciful rumors that were like an aura around the name of Jensen's Planet. Either Jory Jensen himself had talked very freely in his cups, or Longstaffe's laboratory personnel were not nearly as security minded as he was. Each tale she heard was taller than the last; each started from the concept of a magic tree and went from there—with only one saving grace, that no one really believed a word of it, not even those who told the best tales. She had chased the story all over Shangri-La's diverse panderings to wealthy pleasure, and it was, again, like the fabulous Indian Rope-Trick. It was always someone else who had had it at first hand, never the speaker. With the passage of time, the accumulation of repetitions and variations—and her own inner distaste for the frivolous role she had to assume—she had come to disbelieve the whole thing, despite Longstaffe's seriousness, and her trip back to Luna had been meant as her moment to declare it nonsense. Only *then* did she find it.

She had a drowsy image of Admrial Longstaffe's weathered face as she broke it to him that there was a man on the planet who had been living with the tree and its lesser relations for years. She tried to imagine his dismay and anger and it didn't work. Somehow the old man's face turned green, and scarlet flowers blossomed from his ears. He leaned across his desk and nipped her with lobsterlike claws, snarling. . . .

"Don't just lie there smirking. Wake up and do something. Wake up."

Joe's quiet voice splintered her dream, and she stirred drowsily as he called, "Time to start out again, ma'am. You want a bite and fresh up?"

"Oh! Mmmm!" She stretched and sat up. There was just enough light to see. "This is the life," she sighed incautiously. "I haven't slept like that since I was a little girl."

"Make the most of it then; it isn't going to last much longer."

"You really don't like people, do you, Joe?" She stirred and went as far as the river-bank to splash her face with the stingingly cold water. He had a kernel all ready to share with her by the time she was done.

"Got nothing against individuals," he corrected, "it's only when they group up into a thing called society that the devil is born."

"The devil? Personified evil?"

"That's what I mean, all right. It always surprises me that the same people who will agree that society is an entity, a thing other than the people who comprise it—those same people boggle at the idea that good and bad can be similarly regarded as entities."

"It's a thought," she mused through a mouthful. "Society is something sociologists have accepted for a long time—measured its dynamic and formulated rules about it. But I must confess I had never thought of gods and devils in the same style. What particular devil had you in mind?"

"We can go into that some other time," he said. "You have things to learn right now. In about an hour we'll break free of timber and then the green belt altogether. And we will be in danger, as well as being cold."

"Something Friendly can't handle?"

"Right. The cold slows him down a bit. That's why I

want to be into the pass and going through by noon, to get the best of the daylight and sun for him, keep him awake."

"That makes sense. Just what will we be up against?"

He rose, gripping his spear, and they set out through a gray light rapidly turning golden-green. "There's the arrow birds. You know about them. And there are browsers and mountain cats. Those are just my names for 'em. The browsers are huge—anything up to thirty feet long—and eat green stuff, grass, bushes and such—and they know exactly how far into the green belt they can wander before they bite off something too big to chew up."

Selena felt an uneasy tingle along her spine at the idea of massive herbivores accustomed to doing battle with sentient plants. "It must be fun for them," she suggested, "going to nibble at a succulent bunch of leaves and have it try to nibble back."

"Not a lot of fun for us if we run into a bunch of them. They're strong, and all armor-plated around the head and muzzle, and the front feet are clawed like scythes; and they're always hungry—will eat anything they can get hold of—including each other's carcasses."

"What's the strategy for them?" she asked, and he nodded approvingly.

"Depends. Basic precaution is to pick a way that leads in between boulders and rocks, someplace narrow—when you can, that is. And that way they can't come close enough to harm, anyway. Failing that, all you can do is keep a keen ear open all the time and be ready to run like hell for cover. They're slow starters, but they can work up a clip." He let it rest as he negotiated a small gully and an ice-cold stream. He took up the account when they had gained the far side.

"Mountain cats are something else again. There aren't many, which is all the good news. The rest is completely bad. They come about the size of a tiger, maybe smaller, and are always and ever killing mad. Like the browsers, they are always hungry, and that's the one weakness they have. They kill and eat—and nothing will turn them from eating until it's all gone. They have all the teeth and claws any animal ever had and then some. And they almost always lurk high, so they can drop down on their prey. On the ground they wouldn't get much fun out of tangling with a browser, they'd just get tromped."

"And what's the strategy with them?"

"It's tricky," he admitted. "The best bet is to stay right away from overhangs of any kind—but you can't always do that if you're picking narrow trails to baffle the browsers."

"Difficult?" she queried. "It sounds insane to me. Joe, you've made this trip a time or two, obviously, on your own—with just a spear and a knife?"

"The spear," he said, "is just a symbol, I guess. Only thing I ever use it for is to pick fruit sometimes—or to lean on. I've never killed anything with it. Never tried to. All I aim for is to keep out of the way." He leaned into a steep rise, at the top of which the bushes were scantier; there were no trees ahead. "The way I see it," he said, "I'm the interloper here. This is their planet, what right have I to kill them?"

"That may suit you," she retorted, "but—I hope you won't mind—any arrow bird, browser, or mountain cat that shows any sign of being a threat to me had better be able to move faster than I can push the stud on my rifle."

"That's your privilege," he admitted evenly. "We better look out for some thorn hooks now, and I'll give you a hint or two on how to drape this stuff so it will maintain your temperature. That breeze has a bite in it."

It was more than a bite. Sharpened by the rapid change from close jungle heat, it felt to her like knives scraping past; she was eager to learn how to use the hooking thorns to arrange the fleecy material to its best advantage. It was best, he explained, to wrap it around in many layers, but to leave arms, shoulders and legs free for movement. A dangling length between the shoulder blades would come in later for a hood.

"And make it loose," he emphasized. "Might feel insecure and breezy, but it will cuddle up by itself if you get real cold."

"Colder than this?"

"This is just cool, on the skin. Once we move that will pass off. You ready?"

She was, and they went on, soon into bleak rocky terrain where all there was to see of life was the stubborn greenish moss on the rocks. He went ahead now, holding out his spear butt first like a guide rod, tapping ahead.

"Forgot to mention the snakes," he explained. "They move

out of the way if they have the chance, but they object to being stood on."

She pretended to accept the explanation, but it didn't fool her at all, and she marched at his back with her beamer ready, just in case.

ELEVEN

THEY MADE THE peak of the pass as near to noon as she could estimate by the sun, precisely on schedule and without coming too close to any hazards. The peaks on either side, far from providing any kind of shelter, seemed to funnel what had been a constant breeze into a gale. Her extremities complained, but the rest of her was cozily warm inside the creeping fiber. There, she mused, was an idea that, properly exploited, would get someone a considerable fortune. She tried tactfully suggesting it to him.

"When other people start coming here, Joe," she said, "as they will, what will you do? Establish claim, or move out?"

"Hadn't thought much about it. I won't leave, that's for sure. I'll get by."

The edge on his tone warned her to leave that topic. She tried another one on him.

"How did you happen to find this place?"

"I'd rather not talk about it."

"All right. What were you before you came here?"

"Nobody much. Just one more in the rat race, I guess. Wondering what it was all about, what it's all for?"

"Did you find any answers?"

"Not until I came here and had time to think things out. This place is real; it makes sense. Plants don't spend their time trying to be something else. They just live and grow and mind their business."

She took the hint and saved her breath for the climb, and to pump blood against the increasing chill. They had seen a herd of browsers, but fortunately from a safe distance. They were graceless creatures, lumbering mountains of gray-green scales and matted fur—and even while she was imagining what that combination would do to the biologists who maintained that no animal could have fur and scales at the same time—she saw the herd attacked by a stray covey of arrow birds. She was surprised. Big and lumpish they might be, but they could wheel fast enough in their tracks when threatened.

"It's the fool birds that don't learn," he pointed out, as they hid and watched. "Even if they don't smash up on those scales, they don't pack enough punch to kill one of those wallopers."

She saw one diving lizard hit and penetrate right up to its head in a browser's matted fur. And before anything else could happen the mighty fang-filled maw came around and snapped, and there was just the stump of the beak there, still buried in meat.

"But surely," she suggested, ordering her stomach to behave, "enough wounds like that and the biggest beast must go down?"

"Right. And his buddies will eat him, and any arrow birds that try to carve something for themselves. The only time the birds win is if there's a swarm of them, or they happen on a youngster on his own."

It had been an arduous trip. According to him they were over the worst and it was all down hill. She could have admired the view, the sweeping panorama of forest, mountainside and distant sea, had it not been far too cold for hanging about. Besides which she was hungry and said so.

"Me, too," he admitted. "There's plenty of food down there, so let's get on; the sooner we get back among the trees the better I'll like it—and Friendly. He don't care for altitude at all."

She hadn't seen the little blue flower head in some hours. Cowering away from the abnormal chill and the thin air, it had long since retreated from his hair and was safely snuggled somewhere inside his woolly garment. She had a pretty good idea just how dependent he was on the flower's senses, and how uneasy he must be with them partially blunted, yet he showed no sign of hesitation as they began the steep descent.

They were scrambling down a gorge that showed every sign of becoming a young valley. The river in its cleft leaped and chattered as if in a hurry to meet it's fate among the green that was tantalizingly close below. Selena came up to his shoulder, in a moment when he was casting about for the next drop, and declared, "I tend not to like people who abandon things—a chase, a race, a duty, things like that. I'd much rather someone rocked the boat than jumped out."

"It's a point of view," he admitted as he crouched and scrambled down another ledge. "Lots of people have claimed that it's the malcontents and misfits in society who make all the changes—and they claim that's a good thing—keeps progress progressing."

"And there's something wrong with that?"

"I didn't say so. All I know is that if you keep right on butting your head against a brick wall, you'll end up with a concussion. The wall won't change any. Mark Twain said, once 'If at first you don't succeed, try, try again, and then quit. No point in being foolish!' If I don't fit into society, why should *it* change to make room for *me?*"

"Why shouldn't *it?*" she retorted. "The ideal society should be such that people do fit into it."

"When I hear about one of those maybe I'll go."

"You're a difficult man to like," she complained, bracing herself and leaping down after him. The gorge was getting quite deep now. "You have all sorts of admirable qualities, but you're so prickly."

"You should quit feeling sorry for me."

"You can feel that? I'm sorry, I don't—look, Joe"—she dredged up one of her favorite gambits—"just think about a little grain of sand that gets into an oyster shell and sets up an irritation—and then what happens? A pearl."

"Great—now tell me what the oyster thinks about it."

"You're impossible! You could have been successful at all sorts of things if you had put your mind to it; you know that."

"It's my life," he snorted, and plunged on ahead of her, around a bend in the gorge. Exasperated, she tramped after him, around the corner and into the most foul stench she had ever met. He got it at the same time and froze.

"Cat," he muttered. "Close, too."

She heard him, but her attention was held by the more immediate danger ahead. Up the gorge in lumbering flight came three of the browsers, two large ones and a baby about nine or ten feet long. Now he heard and felt them, and flattened against the rock-wall.

"They're running away from a cat!" she cried, seeing the slinking yellow-furred shape where it bounded hungrily in chase of meat.

"Right into another one. He's waiting here. Can you see him?"

She glanced up and about rapidly and was just in time to see a snarling fury launch itself from a ledge directly above, clawed feet wide and ready to slash and rend. She swung her beamer and fired at the beast. She heard the echoes of its scream and saw it crash into the rock wall where he was standing with his spear braced. Man and mortally wounded animal went down in a thrashing tangle.

"Lie still!" she yelled, and aimed again, seeing the cat's body burn. Then the lumbering monsters were too close to ignore; they couldn't stop even if that idea could have penetrated their thick wits in time. She dropped to a knee and leveled the rifle, drilling a hole through the little one in front. She saw it lurch and skid into a heap. The others ran into the body, whoofed with the impact, and immediately forgot their panic and began to eat it. Sickened by the sight of them, she shot both—but they did not die immediately.

The yellow pursuer caught up and sprang onto one of the big browsers. She lowered her beamer and moved cautiously to where Joe lay dreadfully still with the dead mountain cat sprawled on top of him.

"Joe?" she whispered. "Are you conscious?"

There was no reply, and she crept still closer, not taking her eyes off the grisly feast for one moment. The noise from the struggle between cat and browser was painful; the steep gorge caught and amplified the screech of the cat and the rumble of the browser. She shook her head, took careful aim, and blasted the cat first, crisping it into silence. Then she shot the two browsers, steeling herself to hold down the lever until there was no possible doubt.

Her stomach lurching, she grasped the dead cat's fur and heaved at it until she had Joe uncovered enough to be able to investigate. There was blood on him, and scratches, none of which looked serious—and he was unconscious, but, as far as she could tell, that was only the effect of a blow on the head. She struggled to free him from the cat altogether; and then she took a good breath and tried to remember everything she had been told about how to lift and handle an unconscious body. He stirred.

"Huh? . . . What? . . . Holy jumping jets, my head!"

"You must have struck it against the rock when the cat fell on you. Don't move yet, I haven't had time to examine properly—can you feel if there's anything else?"

"There's a stink." He kept his eyes closed and made a tentative movement or two. "I guess I'm all right. Bruised, nothing more than that. What happened, anyway?" She told him, briefly, and he shook his head as if to deny something. "I owe you my life, I guess. I'm grateful, but I'm sorry you had to kill them all."

"What else could I have done?" She watched him sit up and touch himself where the bloodstains were. "We were right in the track of the things."

"I suppose you're right." He reached around and gathered his spear, yanking to free it from the carcass of the dead cat. There was distaste on his face. "First time this thing has ever had blood on it," he said. And she gave way to irritation.

"Excuse me for living!" she snapped. "You may not value your life all that much, but I do mine, and I was looking after it. Do you mind?"

He got to his feet, stretching gingerly, then made his way down to where the stream lashed at the bend in the track, plunging in and squatting down in it to clean himself. She shivered in sympathy, but he made no sign of feeling the chill. After a while he stood again, shook himself like a dog, and rejoined her.

"We'd better get on," he said, and they went on and down, after scrambling past the odorous carcasses. She felt ruffled and knowing that he was tuned in on her feelings didn't help any. She made a point of changing the power pack on her beamer and keeping the spent one for future recharging.

"Now look," she said at last, unable to repress her indignation any longer. "It's all very fine and good to be averse to killing things. I would go along with that myself most of the time. But when it comes to self-defense—"

"To a choice between you and them, you mean?"

"If you want to put it that way, yes."

"I've been here a long time—four years, according to you. I have never had to kill anything yet."

"How many times have you made this trip to the Tree?"

"Twenty, maybe. I haven't counted."

"Well, all I can say is you've been lucky."

"Maybe. I prefer to keep out of the way of trouble."

"They kill each other anyway!"

"I know. But this is their world. We're interlopers. You know, if you take the long view, mankind is an interloper anyway. Wherever we go we interfere and change and mess things up, playing about with powers and forces we don't understand—upsetting nature—fouling it."

"Oh, well," she sneered. "That's about as far as you can go, isn't it? Now you want to opt out of the whole human race."

"Wish I could. I reckon I'd be better off as a plant."

"Do you, indeed! Then, for Heaven's sake why don't you settle down where we're going, along with your precious Tree, and live right there—instead of on the other side of the mountain?"

"You'll know why soon enough. Getting warmer. We'll be there in about three hours or so."

TWELVE

IN LESS THAN an hour they were into scrubby grass and bushes. The sun was warm, the breeze only a gentle breath. The little blue flower came out of hiding and settled itself around his neck and over an ear as if peering ahead. The relief of tension was as tangible as putting down a heavy load. Selena wasn't sure whether it was her own relief—for the mix-up with the stampeding browsers and the murderous cats had shaken her more than she cared to admit—or whether it came from the strange pair she was traveling with. Joe showed nothing on his face, of course, but there was an easier spring in his step. And as for the small flower, she had quite accepted it as an independent entity, more so because it never turned its one-eyed blue stare on her now, but kept its attention ahead.

Analyzing her own feelings was getting to be her way of passing the time, as all attempts to strike a conversation with Joe seemed to lead straight into differences of opinion. This positive awareness of reduced tension, now; could it be that something of the peculiar sensory ability of the plant life was rubbing off on her? She took an internal look at it and had to admit that she had a definite feeling of welcome from the tangled greenery they were now passing through. And she felt affectionate towards the plants, too. There had been little of nature, the wide open spaces, wind-on-the-heath kind of thing in her life. Earth was rapidly running out of that kind of luxury in any case, and most of her adult life had been spent in arduous conditions where the opportunities for contemplating the harmonies of nature were strictly confined to staring at stars and more or less forbidding environments.

"Joe," she called him, all at once. "Hold on just a minute. I've not seen one like this before. Look."

He came back a step or two to contemplate a thick bush that was laden with bulbous and juicy-looking berries, each about the size of a big Earth grape, but golden yellow in color.

"They look delicious," she confessed. "Are they edible, do you know?"

"You can eat 'em," he admitted, "but go easy with them. They pack a punch like neat alcohol. In fact, most of the saps and juices I've run into have that effect. I don't know the chemistry of it, only the effect."

"Hangovers you've had?" she suggested, and he shook his head, not rising to her mild wit.

"They don't do that. But they will make you falling-down stinko if you eat too many. Watch it."

"I will," she promised, and approached the bush with caution and a mental request. Would it mind if she took some? It didn't seem to, and she collected several laden sprays, tasting one as she stepped out to overtake him. The grape-appearance was deceptive. It was more like a tomato inside; the flavor was delightful—and powerful, reminding her of a liqueur. Something like Cointreau? She tried another and a warm glow grew in her stomach, warning her that he had not spoken idly. She thought she could handle just one more, and she did. *What a quiet and pleasant place* *this is! If only one could live here, starting from scratch. Forget the past. Pretend it had never existed—*she stopped and shook her head in mild irritation as her wraparound slithered into dangling folds for the fourth time.

It was loose and floppy, no matter how she tried to pin it into place with the thorn hooks. She was trying to keep it as a two piece, one band about her bosom and shoulders, the other like a skirt, but the stuff kept snaking away, curling back and coming undone.

"I'm too hot for it," she muttered, "that's the trouble," and she had a sudden mental image of this freak material made into a dress and worn by some unsuspecting female who happened to walk into somewhere hot. *My God!* she thought, *it would just fall off, all by itself!*—and the thought pushed a giggle up into her mouth and it spilled over into a shake of laughter—until she caught herself in sudden apprehension. She shook her head violently.

This won't do. I'm close to being stoned! And he did warn me! I'm a fool! She breathed hard, ordered her whimsical faculties to behave, and took the traitorous silky fiber in both hands, hooks and all.

"I don't need you. I can always get more, if I have to. Goodbye; thank you for keeping me warm when I needed it."

She dropped the bundle by the side of the track—what she hoped was the track—and set out to catch up with him. She couldn't see or hear him, but she knew where he was, and she hurried. The giggles came again, but she swallowed them down and came up about three paces clear of his broad back, and marched demurely along as if nothing was in any way unusual. A few minutes farther on she saw another bush, this time ablaze with scarlet flowers, and she couldn't resist the urge to catch one big one and twist it into her hair over her ear. Just to show him she was quite unconcerned, that was all. Ten paces more, and he stopped.

"You're wearing a flower," he accused. "Why?"

"Why not?" she retorted. "Does it bother you? Is it dangerous?"

"No, to both those. Bothers Friendly a bit, though."

"Oh!" She thought that over, and malice came into her mind. "Maybe he doesn't care for this particular shade of blue?"

"Colors don't have anything to do with it, ma'am. You want to look like a flower, that's your privilege." He didn't shrug, but it was there in his tone. He turned and led on, leaving her to follow, as usual. In a little while her small jest seemed sour, and she withdrew the flower from her hair and let it fall discreetly. *Those damned grape things, and on an empty stomach, too!* That thought stimulated the sensation and she really was hungry.

They were well into the forest by the time he called another halt; there was no need to explain this time. Not only could she see the bed-and-breakfast tree ahead, she had been sensing it for some six or seven minutes earlier. That realization made her thoughtful as they gathered a meal and squatted to enjoy it properly. She blessed the fact that he was the sort of person with whom one could be silent without provoking a lot of questions. It gave her time to think through her sensations and arrange them. Then she brought out the problem for him to comment on.

"I knew this tree was here before we got to it," she told him. "And I think I am beginning to sense you—your reactions, at least. Do you suppose something of the peculiar magic of this place is infecting me, or is it mental extension—practice, I mean."

"I don't know about the tree," he muttered, taking her question quite literally and seriously, as she had known he would. "That could be just wishful thinking, because you had an appetite. As for reading me, that could be just cues and learning—tone of voice, expression, attitudes and posture. You can do a lot with that, sometimes without knowing it."

"Now you're being evasive. Do you know anything at all about basic psychology?"

"Some. I've read up on it. A man has plenty of time to—" He let that rest and changed the subject a little. "You could be barking up a tree that isn't there, if you'll excuse the allusion, ma'am. I told you, these plants are not intelligent—not as we define it. If you want to be clinical about it, no plant has a brain, or anything anyway resembling a brain."

"That," she retorted, "is no argument at all. We know quite a bit about the brain, these days, enough to realize that the old notion about the brain being the seat of consciousness is hard to maintain."

72

"Don't see how you can avoid it," he came back, showing interest. "When you put out the brain, everything else is out."

"But the whole body is you. The whole body is intelligent and alive. The brain is just a part, a special part no doubt, but only a part. You aren't *you* with just a brain—it's a relay center, but it doesn't make experiences, or thoughts either, really. If you have any skills at all you must know that your body has them. A plant doesn't need our kind of brain because it has no need to maintain mobility, to be constantly dealing with changing environment. But the whole-body intelligence can be there, just as it is in us. And it can be just as intelligent as us—only it doesn't talk about it."

"And we can understand and deal with abstractions. A plant can't ever do that if, as you say, it is material-intelligent—just a recorded memory of its own sensations."

"I didn't say it like that, but you have a point. Yes, I suppose we are all the result of what has happened to us."

"Plus what we have learned from everyone else, and what they've all learned, and it goes on." He discarded a section of husk, and added, "A plant can only know its own small world and nothing else at all, whereas a person knows a whole history of the human race merely by learning how to talk."

"Yes," she admitted, and scowled.

He took up the last bit of his fruit meal and began to gnaw it. Her thoughts went along a new tack now, a surprising one for her. In her hectic twenty-five years of life Selena had come to know that she was every bit as good as anyone else and far superior to most. She had come to accept that as a matter of course. Now, in a few short hours, she had been defeated and made to look amateurish at almost everything by this strange man. She discovered that she didn't really mind—because he didn't lean on it or take advantage of it. Her curiosity, never very far from the surface, blazed into renewed heat and suggested a strategy.

"Joe," she said gently. "As we're just sitting here for a bit, may I touch your hand again? Please? I just want to know whether the plant life here sings the same song, speaks the same language as the others did, back there."

He looked at her, his curiously bright eyes very keen.

Then, without a word, he extended his left hand so she could reach and clasp his fingers. In that simple contact the magic came once more, only stronger and more vividly. Instinctively she closed her eyes, and held her breath at the wonder of it. It was so like mighty music, yet utterly soundless, not in her ear at all. She felt great booming organ notes from the trees; a rushing running obbligato of violin-whispering and gossiping from the bushes and climbing creepers, trails of silver sound; bell-like chimes that were flowers; and the scurrying piccolo busy-body shrillness of the grass. And then, faint and far away, something caught her mental ear and held it: a silver horn-note, an invitation, both a plea and promise in one. That call stirred her all the way down inside to depths she never knew she had. She opened her eyes and stared at him.

"What's that?" she breathed. "Something a long way off, calling to me?"

"You asked me, some time back, whether Pardoe would be able to find the Tree—one tree, out of all these millions. I said he would. Now you know."

"That's the Tree, that call?"

"That's it. Couple of hours away yet. Call it fifteen miles. And that's just its normal curiosity, not stirred up. It doesn't know you're here, not yet. When it finds out—" He let the sentence die unfinished and she released his fingers hurriedly.

THIRTEEN

"It will find out about you, discover that you are here. And when it does, it will call you. If Pardoe runs true to form, he will do his looking with a chopper, from above, and it will find out about him a lot faster than it will about you. Can't miss—and it will call him, too."

"Call?"

"Oh yes, it can put the pressure on. Not the way you heard it; that was idle—dreaming, you might say. Once it gets stirred, though—"

Selena felt a chill tickle the back of her neck and her

spine. He must have sensed it, for he put on his teeth-baring smile.

"I don't know whether you're right to be scared, or not. I could say not—that you're in no danger. I could say the Tree won't harm you. It's just curious about anything new and different, that's all. I could say that, and it would be the truth as I know it. But I might be wrong, too. What I can say is that the Tree never did me any harm at all— just the reverse. But I can't expect you to believe that. In the final analysis, I suppose it comes down to what kind of a person you are."

"And what sort of person you are, too," she said. "That's something I don't know, Joe. I've seen you, heard you, watched you—but how do I really know what you are, inside?"

"That's the oldest and still unsolved problem in the world."

"Oh now," she denied. "You have an assist. You can detect me; you've admitted it, and demonstrated it, too. You know what I'm feeling. You have even allowed me to know what the plants and trees are thinking and feeling, through your helper. But, every time, I have never been aware of you in that. You've kept yourself out, somehow. Now why would you do that?"

"Just a habit of mine. Don't like being pushy. Don't talk about myself much, either."

"That may be, but without something like that, how do I know what to believe? You may be leading me into a trap of some kind. You could even be a slave of that—that thing, whatever it is!"

She saw the shutters come down over his face again. "You don't have to go any further, ma'am. You can stop right here, or go back. Suit yourself."

"Don't let's start that again. I want to help, and I *can* help, but I have to know what I'm getting into, who I can trust."

"All right. If that's the way you want it, if it will help at all, just this once can't hurt." He held out his hand to her again. She looked at it, at him, and had to drive herself to reach and take his fingers this time. At first there was nothing at all, not even the orchestral vegetation. His face was a guarded mask, his eyes blank—then he started to fade away, to become shadowy and unreal, even as she stared.

Shaken by that impossibility she shut her eyes tight. Now, with a sense of being suspended in mid-air without support, she began to receive him—or something that she felt was him. An in-depth color-sound-emotion blend: a steady flame without heat, the straightness of a sword blade, steel, transparency that was serenity, curiosity without intrusion, fellowship, kinship, and warmth that infused and soothed, that was total self-confidence. Words and inadequate images tumbled over themselves in her mind and she abandoned them impatiently and let the mystery that was him flood in and become known to her.

Then he took his hand away, and he went away like a quick-fading image in sand. She opened her eyes.

"Never did anything like that before—only once," he muttered. "I hope it helped you, ma'am."

It seemed that she hadn't breathed in a long while. She caught up on it, trying to clutch at a fading impression of something wonderful, but it erased itself, leaving only an afterglow.

"I don't know about help, Joe. I don't know how much of that to believe, but I'm going to accept it just as it came and trust it—and you. You say the Tree won't harm me. All right, I'll accept that. We can go on just as soon as you say."

Without another word he rose and started. She followed, drifting in a half-dream through the luxuriant green, bathed in the scents and senses of murmuring life all around, and utterly bemused. Part of her mind could isolate and cling to one hard fact, that she had been permitted to know one other person in a way she had never believed possible. For her it meant a complete redefining of the term to know, as applied to anyone else. She thought back to the Jory Jensen dossier she had studied. What had it told her? He was born at a certain date in a certain place. He had this, that and the other certificates, degrees and skills. He was so high, of such a color skin and eyes, and weight—and all the rest of it. But it had not told her what sort of a person he was because there was no one to know that, nor words to express it. But she knew, now, exactly what sort of a person Joe was.

She knew him, and it was a wonderful, a humbling thing. It was even more humbling, in the midst of the warmth that was remembering him, to realize that he must know her just as completely. Did she come out of the experience as handsomely? She went deep down into self-examination and doubted it and felt herself a mass of submerged frustrations and petty bitternesses, conceits and contradictions. Then she thought of the blue flower; that flower was the key.

She imagined how it might be if someone could gather seeds of the flower and propagate them far and wide, making them available to the scattered and seething millions of suffering humanity. *The barriers would come down in ruins. People would really be able to know each other. Away would go all the inadequacy of signs and symbols and clumsy words, the deceptions and half-truths. Personalities revealed*—and then her inborn common sense called a shuddering halt.

Would that be so good? She wondered. Would it be wonderful to encounter a mind and personality like—Buck Pardoe or Scorpia Martine?—or, indeed, any one of hundreds of undesirable characters she could call to mind out of a lively past? Shrinking from that, she modified the thought a little. *Why select the known bad ones? Wouldn't it be just as shocking to unveil ordinary people? Nice people? Wouldn't it be something like entering unannounced a bedroom or bathroom? Invasion of privacy!* She grew so immersed in this line of speculation that the matter-of-fact world went by her unheeded. It was with a sense of shock that she suddenly realized that she was standing quite still.

Real-time awareness came to her in discreet bits.

Now that she was paying attention, a presence knocked gently but insistently at the door of her mind. It came in as soon as she was aware of it. It was strong yet gentle, warm, embracing, promising, inviting, and almost saying, "Come to me, let me know you, let me know all about you. Come!"

She retained just enough selfhood to flash an urgent appeal to Joe, who stood waiting for her. He shrugged helplessly.

"You can turn around and walk away if you want to. But you don't want to, knowing you. I don't think it will harm you—but I have to say just this. Back there a bit we were talking about devils and gods, the personifications of abstractions. I can define one devil for you that bites hard into all civilized people. Call it willing self-deception, the ability to think of rational excuses for all the stupid and wrong things we do and believe in."

With an effort she detached her mind from that insidious call, and shook her head at him. "Is that relevant now?"

"I think so. Deception's a nice devil. He helps you believe yourself, helps you kid yourself that you're not really bad at all, that all the evil and wicked things you think and feel and do are not really bad at all—just force of circumstances, or misunderstanding by other people. A comforting devil to have. But the Tree doesn't know about such things. Without knowing, it casts out devils."

"That can't be bad," she said, and smiled, and then surrendered herself to the insistent and urgent call in her mind. She went into the cool stream, across it and up the bank beyond, passing Joe with another smile. Over the ridge were scattered bushes of all kinds in profusion, so that she had to pursue a winding path, weaving in and out but always following that Lorelei call. It grew stronger and more confident, throwing her inner emotions back into childhood, creating for her the image of father-mother benevolence and vast affection. There was an almost tangible embrace and welcome. Then there were no more bushes, just a clear space and a hanging green veil. She paused, mildy curious until she saw what it was. The Tree was inside somewhere, like the central pole of some immense tent, and this veil was the drooping fronds of its outermost branches.

She put out her hand to part the curtain, but it drew aside for her, opening a lane in the green and inviting her in. Beyond the curtain itself there was a cool turf-floored expanse that gave her the impression of a church, of being imbued with reverence. It was immensely high, seeming to fade away into a sunlit green haze. The trunk itself was large—by any standards an old and enormous forest giant. Selena was not awed by the size alone. She had walked in sequoia groves, among trees that would dwarf this one, but none of those had ever impressed her with such majesty. The vast trunk, some twenty feet through, was dark green, almost black; and it was glossy, without a single branch to interrupt its soaring rise until the eye had followed it at least a hundred feet into the green haze.

Her irrational fears had vanished. There was no hazard here, only a vast and curious benevolence, patiently serene. She stood for a while just bathing in the presence, feeling it like a caress on her skin. Then she remembered the beamer and charges that she carried, and felt wrong about them. Apologies came to her mind as she peeled off the straps and laid her weapons on the turf. Then the call came so plainly that there could be no error, and she advanced, put out her hands and laid her palms flat on the trunk of the Tree.

As when Joe had revealed himself to her, the outlines of sight began to blur, fade and dissolve, and she closed her eyes. Time hung still; existence became unreal, unimportant. There was a tingle in her fingers and arms as if the Tree itself rippled and moved. A phrase came to her mind out of the long ago, *"Goodness went out of me!"* Who had said it? It was as if everything she was and ever had been flowed out of her through her palms and into the Tree. At first, it was good, a tingle of pleasure and greeting. Then it was lassitude and misgiving—and fear. Shaking waves of dark fear swelled up in her and became terror that drowned her into panic. Aghast, clinging to that cool trunk, shaking and weak, she felt wave upon wave of stupefying dread, help-lessness and emptiness, as if all her substance were melting away to become nothing.

She clung desperately to the tree as the only real thing in the nightmare; there came pain in rushes and spurts, and the strong soundless music again, shaking and vibrating, tearing her to pieces, ripping small agonies from her body like plucking hairs—and yet there was no hurt, no injury. The pain swept over and through her like a flood, but it was a fire that burned without consuming, that left strength and clarity. Purification—dimly but happily she knew that the flow was not all one way, that something surged back into her from the Tree—something that was good, strong, and bold. The last vestiges of cowardice and dread washed out in that comforting flow. She knew, as plainly as if it had been shouted in her ear, that she was now whole, healthy and clean. And this the Tree had done for her, and to her, and she was thankful in a way that made an everlasting bond between it and her.

With a silent but sincere gratitude she lowered her hands and turned, to see Joe standing a few feet away, watching her. She felt gratitude to him, too, and a sense of sharing something wonderful with him. She put out her hand in greeting, started to go to him, and her legs folded under her, the glade and everything in it fell away into darkness and silence.

FOURTEEN

WHEN SHE CAME back to consciousness she was stretched out flat on turf and able to stare up into the vast vault of the Tree. She was quite at ease, knew where she was, had no fear, and just lay there in peace, savoring the rare pleasure of being completely comfortable and happy. The completeness of it was in itself remarkable, and she was just beginning on that thought when she grew aware of a low muttering, quite close. She sat up and turned to look; there was Joe. He squatted before the Tree with his hands out to touch it, and he was talking to it. She wrinkled her brow at that, for a moment, but then let it go. Surely speech, she thought, was neither necessary nor of any use, but maybe it helped him with mental imagery. She lay back on an elbow and returned to contemplation of her own well-being. She looked up as he came padding across the grass to her and sank into a squat by her side.

"How do you feel?" he asked. She smiled.

"You know I can't describe it. I've read quite a lot by people who have had striking spiritual experiences, and it always comes to the same thing—it can't be described."

"That's in the Tao," he said unexpectedly. "If you can describe it, that's not it. I think that is what the Bible passage means—the peace of mind that passes all understanding. Something like that."

"I am through being surprised at anything you say, Joe. After that experience, nothing will surprise me. I feel as if I had been taken apart, molecule by molecule, and put back together again properly, the way I should have been all along. Isn't it crazy?"

"Say it like that and it is, but it's true. That's what I meant about casting out devils. We humans carry about with us all sorts of lies and illusions to preserve us against the sometimes unpleasant realities. That's why so very few people are really fit and healthy, and well. They don't know the right way to live, which is determined by the design of the body itself."

"I think it's more than that. I know something you don't, perhaps. Scientists have investigated the seeds of that Tree, and I know this about their results: those seeds grow and produce plants that have the power to take a construct from a human mind and create it in solid reality. It can deliver what you want."

"So?"

"So I suppose everyone has some kind of meaningful image of what he or she would like to be, a kind of super-ego picture of what we could be. And I think the Tree uses that as a working base."

"Maybe." He sounded doubtful. "It has limitations. It's only a tree, after all."

"You mean, this euphoria could be some kind of illusion in itself? That's a possibility I hadn't considered—hypnosis and suggestion."

"How do you tell the difference?"

"Well." She pondered. "If it really is repair and restructure—I have a scar or two. Mementoes of a lively past. Excuse me." She searched for a scar—and there was no scar.

"It's real, all right. Instant healing!"

"Not instant," he corrected. "It took an hour for you, maybe more. And maybe not healing, either. I told you, it's mental pictures it gets. If that's true then it fixes you up the way you want to be, as far as possible. And that's not always good, is it?"

"I suppose not," she agreed, and fled hastily from any possible revelation of her vanity. "But what do you mean by limitations?"

"Never mind. Look, we'd better get out of here to where we can keep an ear out for Pardoe and the others. This place is close to being soundproof, and Friendly isn't any help either. He's a relative of the Tree, you see, and completely paralyzed all the time he's here."

"Sort of 'Keep quite while Grandad is talking,' you mean?"

"That's about the size of it." He rose and she went up with him as if new springs had been fitted into all her sinews. The delight of it was like wine and she had to fight to remain calm.

"I confess I'd forgotten all about Pardoe," she admitted as they left the glade, through the curtain of leaves and into the reddish glow of late afternoon. They headed for the stream. "Do you think he will harm the Tree?"

"I think so. I'm not sure. The only thing I have in mind is to stop him from getting at it, somehow. You're pretty good with that beamer."

"Yes, but if you think I'm going to shoot him down out of the sky, think again."

"I know. He'll have your friends aboard. He's no fool. He will figure that you value their lives."

"And I do, at least as much as my own, or yours."

"As much as the whole of the rest of humanity?" he challenged. She started to be angry with him. Then she was struck rigid as he threw her anger right back at her, as positively and unarguably as if it had been a ball.

"Good Heavens!"

"Right," he said grimly. "That's just one of the tricks I've learned from that Tree. You had some before, remember? When you tried to go for me, out by your ship? You probably thought that I hit you with something, and, in a way, I did, but all it was—I threw your own mental attack right back at you."

"Why wait until now to demonstrate—this ability?"

"Because, to do it, I have to touch you mentally to sense what you're doing, so I can reverse it. And—before—I didn't care to do that."

"Very delicately put. In other words, I was repulsive?"

"Put it like that, if you want. The point is, it can be learned. All I did was ask for it. I needed it, or so I thought, to protect myself in a place like this. I don't use it now, and you can see why."

"Yes, but I've lost your point somewhere. What has this to do with Pardoe and my friends?"

"And humanity, remember? Your trouble is, you're stuck

on yourself. You're Selena Ash; your old man's a big wheel; maybe you've all the right in the world to think you're it."

"You won't make me angry again."

"Not trying to. I'm trying to tell you something. You've had a fumble or two, a knock or two, since you got here. But it didn't teach you a thing. That was just alien plants and such. You didn't feel you needed any help. You're still way up there."

"I take it you do have a point."

"Coming to it. Even when you met the Tree, you just swapped curiosity with it and got yourself a swift check-over and repair, that's all. No—you hold still and listen." Now he had somehow placed an invisible clamp on her, and her back hair began to lift at this further evidence of power.

"When I first came to the Tree I needed help in the worst way. That's how I found out what it could do. I thought I needed protection from the plants, and it gave me powers—you've seen some. Now I know a better way, by being friendly, but that's by the side. I thought I needed a weapon, and I had to explain to the thing just what that was, because it's only a tree, remember? And it grew me a spear. You've seen it. I carry it about to remind myself what a damn fool I was. This knife, though, was sensible. It grew that, too—for me."

He paused, and she began to understand what he was trying to explain. He went on, still calmly grim. "Let's run through it again. The Tree will do for you whatever you want, as far as it possibly can, as much as it can understand. It doesn't know good from bad or right from wrong. You want the strength of ten men? You want to be fifteen feet tall? You want power? You have only to ask, to want in the right way—the way it can understand—and you've got it. So—I ask you—what do you think Buck Pardoe will do with that? Do you have any idea what desires are squirming in his mind?"

He released the power that held her, but she didn't move. She felt sick as he went on stonily. "What do you think all the crooks, the dregs, the scum of humanity will do with it, when they get it? You've just said that certain scientists have investigated its fruit. That means there can be, and there will be, other Trees—hundreds of them. God alone knows all the tricks this one can get up to. I only know some, but that is enough to convince me that wiping out Buck Pardoe and that woman is a small price to pay, and the lives of your friends, and your life, and mine, aren't much more, against the whole of humanity."

"And I've sent a Dirac," she said emptily. "It's too late to call that back."

"That's the least of our worries," he retorted swiftly. "If I know anything about Space Service, there'll be—hold it!" He halted, grew still and tense like a pointer, turned his head to listen, and the little blue-eyed flower turned with him. "Here they come now," he muttered. "You hear it?"

She strained, and then nodded. Very faintly came the puttering sound of a jetcopter. He breathed hard.

"Right!" he grunted, and went away like a blur. There was no hint or request for her to follow. She picked up her feet and went after him as fast as she could, exulting in her new-found vitality, but soon realizing that he had a turn of speed she had not seen until now. And he seemed to have an unerring instinct for the way through, or around, and she was streaming with sweat as she came up to him at the base of a tree.

"You want in on this?"

"Of course," she panted. "I said I'd help."

"Give me the beamer. I can climb the tree faster with it than you can without."

"Oh, can you, indeed?" Her momentary indignation was wasted as he vanished upwards like a squirrel. She shook her head ruefully and set herself to follow. She managed quite well, but he was out of sight long before she had gained the first few branches. She caught him right at the top, where the tree's limbs were perilously slender and yielding, and squirmed on her stomach along a thin branch to be close to him.

"Over there," he told her unnecessarily, as she had already seen the distant blot of the buzzing craft. "He's quartering. He can't miss. As soon as the Tree gets that noise it will perk up and call him."

She accepted the beamer from his hand, stretched out on the uneasy perch and took tentative aim. It was about twenty-five miles, which was too far for accurate marksmanship.

"I can't do it, Joe. You know that, don't you?"

"I know." He sounded resigned. "Never thought you would. You and me, we're not the kind that can kill in cold blood. Can't help being what we are, I suppose."

"True enough, but let's not abandon all hope yet. I know a trick or two once he gets close enough."

"What kind of trick?"

"How well do you know the terrain about here? Is there somewhere he can land that thing close by? I mean, once he gets the feel of the Tree he will look for somewhere to come down, won't he? Where?"

"Two or three spots. Nearest is a clearing about two miles off, over to the right. Not very big, but enough for what he wants."

"Just one more detail. That's a hybrid craft, isn't it? Part copter, with jet assist?"

"Right."

"Well, if he's close enough, and is about to land, I can clip his wings for him, so that he may be able to get down safely, but he won't get back up again."

"That's a trick, all right. Where'd you learn it?"

"Not in school. I need a firmer branch than this." She backed and let herself down to a stouter limb, settled on it and kept her eyes on the dark machine. On a thought, she called up to him, "Can you let me know when he decides to go down?"

"I'll try. There—he's got the message! Watch him go!" She saw the jetcopter heel over and come swooping towards them, growing bigger rapidly. She could imagine the jubilation in Pardoe's mind at the first solid intimations that the Tree was real. The forward flight halted and the cab oscillated under its winged canopy. She set the rifle for needle focus and full power, set the stock against her cheek, and waited for the right moment.

FIFTEEN

"Just making up his mind to land," Joe advised in an urgent whisper, and she spent an idle thought wishing she could pick up emotions at a distance like that. Then the swaying machine within her sights began to drop, its note changing. She drew a bead on the very edge of the blur that was the rotating blades, pressed the lever, and a fine thread of electric blue sprang out to lose itself in the evening sunlight. At once the flying machine shivered and swayed violently. The stuttering beat became a clamor, and she heard the sudden frantic whine of jets as whoever was at the controls threw in the lifters to prevent a total crash. The black shape bucked crazily and then went down fast. She peered over the sights of her weapon anxiously, but there was no crash.

"Neat," Joe muttered, coming to stand behind her. "He's down all in one piece, and they're all in good shape, but he can't get back up. And it will be dark soon."

"What will he do, sit tight until dawn? I would."

"Never can tell. Depends on how strong the Tree calls him. I reckon our best bet is to get along there and keep an eye on him."

In the dark? The query came to her lips, but she halted it as an idea struck her. He put out his hand for the weapon, and she passed it back to him, wriggling around to see him go down, dropping almost as fast as if he were falling. *I'm just beginning to catch on to all this,* she thought as she followed at a slightly less frantic pace. *If you want to learn how to climb up and down trees, who better to go to than the great white chief of all the trees—and ask?* It was so obvious. It was difficult to adjust to the notion that one could have whatever one wanted, merely by asking. She scrambled and dropped, and then stood by his side. He aimed an arm and moved, but she called him back.

"Can we spare a few minutes to call on the Tree, first?"

"It's out of our way a bit."

"Only a little. And I need help, the kind of help the Tree can give me."

"Thin end of the wedge," he said cryptically. "All right, this way." He went off at a smart pace. She followed, trying to deduce what he had meant. It came to her after a while. One could get hooked on a thing like this. If you can have whatever you want, simply by asking for it, what happens to discipline, and effort, and moral fiber?—and pride of accomplishment, and all the other things humanity had held in high esteem for so long?

"What is it that you want from the Tree? Don't tell me, but think about it."

"Why shouldn't I tell you?"

"Can if you want, but thinking about it is the hard part. Not in words—that's no good. You have to feel it, believe it, present it in the form of an accomplishment—call it faith."

She pondered that as she ducked through the undergrowth at his heels. Longstaffe's words came back. The botanical researchers had believed the seeds were this, or that—and so they were. One must make an image, but how does one make an image of being able to see in the dark? She remembered how the Tree had plucked from her mind her own fond image of being a gorgeous gray-eyed brunet with a flawless complexion and a knock-your-eye-out figure. That was hardly a belief, more an ideal to be hoped for, and a delight now that she had it. Her mental waters grew deep and confused, and she was far from having them cleared by the time they reached the dim serenity of the tree-temple again.

"I need your help," she said, outside the leaf-curtain, "to get this thing right. Look, all I'm after is some way of being able to move at ease in the dark. Perhaps the ability to detect living forms over a long distance the way you do."

"That's out," he rejected instantly. "I don't do that. Friendly does it for me. There are plenty of his brothers around here, but it takes time and practice and you have to develop the relationship."

"Can't I have that power on my own?"

"I doubt it. You're human, like me. We don't have that kind of equipment, so far as I know. What d'you expect, instant miracles? I keep telling you, it's only a tree!"

"You keep confusing me," she retorted. "What if I want my night vision improved, then? That's fully consonant with being human."

"All of that," he agreed acidly. "Only you're forgetting again. No tree, or plant ever *had* eyes or vision or anything like it. I've told you about their sense of space; that they do have. But how can you expect a tree to understand vision?"

"Like red to a blind man," she murmured, and inwardly scolded herself for being so blind. "Never mind, it can't hurt to try. Here goes." She walked through the curtain of leaves and up to the tree, composing her mind as she went, convincing herself that she could see the trunk, the lofty vault above, the branches, all of it plainly and in detail, despite the fact that it was almost totally dark in there. Halting, she revised it just one more time by telling herself that it *was* like that, and then put her hands affectionately on the trunk. Just for a breath there was, again, that sense of something going out of her—and then a warm counter-flow that became a rush, a flood, a bursting feeling—tiny galaxies of sparks erupted and died rapidly in her mind, a barrage of tickling thrills bathed her body and she was giddy. She would have fallen had she not clung tightly to the trunk. She leaned on it, closing her eyes. The all-over tingling subsided slowly.

And she could see the trunk quite plainly. She could see all around it, the grass under her feet and the graceful spreading branches overhead. And she could see Joe, quite definitely, standing there close behind her. *Behind?* She pushed away from the Tree and turned to him, smiling—and then realized her eyes were still shut tight. Opening them, she almost fell at the vertigo inspired by the two different but simultaneous images. By sight he was a hulking object in the gloom, but by this other sense he was there as a person, felt and identified in some delightful and inde-scribable way.

"Give me a minute," she said breathlessly. "This wants some getting used to. And don't ask me to describe it, I can't."

"You got something? You mean it actually did something for your vision?"

"No," she said, very softly because she knew the reason for his urgency. "Not sight. You were probably right about that. But I have something better. Let's go."

It *was* better. With this new perception she could slip through bushes and tangles just as easily as he did, *and* know what was beyond, and all around her too. The dark-ness made no difference at all. She tried it with her eyes shut and it was as if she moved through a living world of bright images, all different and distinct, known and identi-fied exactly as if, in some marvelous way, she could touch them with long and delicate fingers. It was an effort to bring her mind back to more commonplace affairs.

"Do you have any kind of plan in mind?" she asked him.

"Nothing hard, no. Let's find that copter first—see what they are up to. Play it by ear from there. First thing I have in mind is to make sure that machine won't fly, ever again. After that we'll figure out some way of stopping Pardoe from getting to the Tree."

"I can't improve on that. What I don't quite get is why you're so bothered about the Tree itself. You know a lot more about it than I do, of course—" She chopped it off as she sensed the stationary bulk of the machine and four human shapes ahead. Shock waves came from one of them. They went forward together cautiously, making full use of the cover, for there was still enough light to make the risk considerable. Crouched behind a friendly bush, they saw Pardoe grasping a blade and staring at it furiously.

"All four!" he snarled, shoving it violently away. "That's all I need. That was no accident. Somebody took a shot at us."

" 'Way out here?" Miss Martine doubted it.

"What else would fuse the blade tips into globs of metal?" he roared back at her. "Whoever it is"—his voice swelled to a bellow—"you better believe me, one more trick and I burn these two down right away!"

"There's nobody to hear you, Buck."

"Who asked you? You just stay there and keep your burner on the playboys, while I rescue some equipment."

Pardoe scrambled back into the machine, and Joe sighed. "Can't do a thing until he moves out. You say I'm bothered about the Tree itself and that's right. Look, it's a mistake to credit it with too much, as it now is. Sensitive to mental fields. Possessed of certain mimetic powers. That's about it. But alien. I mean, it can't hear. It can detect sounds, sure, but a blown balloon can do that. It can sense light and shade, but not to see. The point is, all the development of those senses is human, and we use our senses because we've been taught how. The Tree hasn't been taught anything. It knows only what it has met and experienced."

"Yes. I can see that."

"And we are the only two humans it has ever met, the only ones it knows. It's had a considerable effect on me, and on you—but we have also had an effect on it. You understand that?"

"Yes, I do." She recalled the sensation of goodness going out, and caught her breath. "Good God! I see what you mean. You're saying the Tree is innocent, naïve."

"That's right. Just like an overgrown child. Now you try and imagine what effect it is going to have when it gets a taste of Buck Pardoe and Scorpia Martine!"

Selena started to ponder the prospect, but before she could get beyond a chill despair Pardoe came boiling out of the craft again.

"You must be out of your mind," Miss Martine expostulated. "Why thrash about in the dark, damn it."

"Because I say so I told you six or eight times already, we have no time to give away. All the time Miss High-and-Mighty Ash is missing there will be somebody—a whole lot of somebodies—looking for her. Maybe it will take them years to find this planet, and then again, maybe it won't. Half the Space Navy is looking for this place right now, and has been looking for a long while; you know what I mean. And maybe somebody has already found it, too, to go by those blades. We don't have any time to sit around and get fat."

"Get fat!" she screeched furiously. "Eaten alive by crazy plants, all my best duds rotted and ruined, two damned invalids to feed and nurse, and now your damned flying eggbox folds up on us—you call that getting fat? And now you expect to march out and find a tree, one tree, in the dark?—with God only knows what skulking in the bushes. You must be out of your mind; you've seen what the crazy things can do!"

"I've seen. You don't have to tell me. It will be just too bad for any plant that tries to get gay with me from here on." Pardoe sounded mean enough to spit acid right back at the surrounding undergrowth. She perceived how the unlikely caravan began to move and felt the first hurt of the plants as Pardoe blasted them to ashes in his path and marched forward.

"That hurts," Selena gasped, and Joe grunted in sympathy.

"Just one more reason for stopping him. Those plants are all my friends. Makes me ashamed to be human. They're almost clear of the craft now. Can you get a bead on it?"

"Just leave it to me." Selena aimed and poured a steady disruptive beam into the machine until it crackled and collapsed.

"That takes care of that," she declared with considerable satisfaction. "Have they noticed anything?"

"Not them. Pardoe is making too much clatter for anybody to notice anything. The way they're headed they should pass close by us. We might as well keep still."

She directed her attention to the oncoming travelers, wincing as Pardoe kept letting go with a heavy-duty blaster to clear a way for himself. *Much more of that*, she thought, *and it won't be so difficult to shoot you down, cold blood or not.*

"Follow my track!" Pardoe commanded, "and if those two drag on their feet just toast 'em up a bit."

"How the hell can you tell which way you're going?"

"You mean to tell me you can't feel it? I always said you were so stuck on yourself you don't know anybody else is alive. Just keep on going, that's all you have to do. I'll take you to it."

SIXTEEN

"WE LIE low, let 'em go by, then I clobber her from the back and we maybe can grab your friends, right? Think you can shoot that beamer out of her hand?" Joe whispered.

"I think so. I'll try to time it for your strike. Careful!"

"I will. You stay right here."

He went away with no more noise than a shadow, but she was able to follow his progress easily.

Behind Pardoe came the captives Delmar and Lacoste, shambling and reeling in acute distress. Each man had his wrists lashed together at his back, and a stout black plastic cable linked them, from the slip-noose about one neck to its counterpart about the other, so that neither man dared stumble and fall for fear of strangulation. There was no sign of any care of nursing, as Miss Martine had claimed, and Selena itched in sympathy as she saw their scars and scratches. Following, looking thoroughly bored and disgusted, came Miss Martine herself, visibly out of humor with the whole situation, but maintaining an alert grip on her beamer.

Joe was behind Miss Martine and ready to strike. Selena

took careful aim and held her breath. Some instinct seemed to warn Miss Martine, perhaps some tiny sound or smell. She stiffened. The spear came down in the same second that she ducked and whirled, and caught her on the arm. She yelled in fright. Selena wriggled frantically, trying to get a clean shot. Miss Martine hoisted her beamer, and down came Joe's spear again, cracking solidly against the weapon. It went spinning away, and in the next second Joe and the woman were grappled and thrashing about in the undergrowth in a confusion of arms and legs.

Up ahead, Pardoe roared in anger, spun around, came galloping heavily back, elbowing the helpless captives out of the way. Miss Martine let out a shrill scream from the tangle and her partner homed in on it. Selena saw his unoccupied hand reach for a fragmentation pistol.

"Get clear!" he roared. "Damn it, Scorpia, get out of the way, let me get a shot at it!"

Selena acted without pause to consider implications. She sent a needle-beam slicing through the cable that linked the captives, then swung and aimed delicately at the heavy-charge beamer which jutted from Pardoe's right hand, now in perfect profile. The lethal metal erupted in a spray of incandescent sparks, and he flung it away from himself frantically, then spun heavily around, snarling, to peer into the gloom. Up came the frag-pistol in his hand, and the night flew apart in thunder as it spat one—two—three—and stopped. His aim was good. Selena heard the slugs rip through the night air where she had been crouched. Then, as they struck, the echoing silence gave way again, this time to a chorus of banshee wails as the lethal fragments sprayed the surrounding darkness.

Face down and still, Selena was able to follow the action quite well. There was another animal screech from Miss Martine, a solid thumping blow, silence—and Joe melting shadowlike into the gloom, leaving her prone. Pardoe came close, kicked her to see if she was conscious, but kept his eyes continually scanning the surrounding gloom.

"Scorpia, you all right?"

She groaned, sat up and rubbed her head.

"Come on, come on," he urged. "What happened? Where'd he go?"

"I don't know, and I don't care, just so long as he stays

gone. He? That was no he, Buck. It was an ape! Wild man of the woods. Something like that. Hey! Leggo my foot, damn it!" She scrambled up rapidly, rescuing her ankle from the grip of a green tendril. "Give that damned shrub a blast, will you? Before it comes after me."

"Some hope," he snarled. "Your so-called ape-man just shot my beamer out of my hand with one of his own. Him, or his friends. Some ape! Use your own."

"If I can find it in the damned dark." Miss Martine stooped complainingly to search, while Pardoe glared a-round into the gloom.

"Damn it!" he growled. "Where'd he go?" and then, giving vent to fury, he loosed off three more thunder-clap shots, and the shrill wails of shattered steel came back. But there were no screams of agony or indications of a hit. "Yah," he snorted. "Got away. Oh, come on, you, and quit that moaning! You and your judo and karate and all that, and you let yourself get jumped—hey!" Surprise choked him for a moment, then the leafy darkness shook to the fury of his cursing as he realized that his captives were gone.

Back by the little knoll from which all the havoc had been done, Selena staggered to a halt and lowered Pierre Lacoste to the ground, gave a thankful sigh of relief.

"Hush now," she warned. "Not a sound. He's too handy with that splinter gun to take chances. Thanks, Joe, for tak-ing Robin. I think he would have been a bit too heavy for me. Let's have that knife—"

A few seconds later the two baffled and battered men were free of their bonds. Lacoste was too far gone to do anything but stare, but Delmar still retained enough spark to peer into the gloom and gasp, "Selena? It is you, isn't it? But who's this character?"

"Call him Joe. He's a friend, on our side. No time to ex-plain just now. Hush. That Pardoe has long ears and a brain. Keep still."

Excitement erupted again below. Miss Martine had found her beamer and something else.

"A spear?" Pardoe demanded incredulously. "Don't tell me we have native tribes on our necks, too."

"That's it, Buck—got to be! We've been jumped by some local tribe, and they've carried off our prisoners." Her agita-tion was plain. "Look, Buck, why don't we go back to the jetcopter and button up until it's light, huh? This stumbling about in the dark, it's crazy. The next thing you know they'll get us, too."

"Anybody who tries to jump me," Pardoe vowed, "will get a gutfull of splintered steel. I don't like this, Scorpia."

"You don't *like* it?"

"That's not what I mean. Use your skull, damn it. Native tribes don't come complete with beamers."

"You sure it was a beamer?"

"What the hell do you think did this?" He waggled the ruined and partly fused weapon under her nose, and she wailed.

"That only makes it worse! Buck, I'm scared. Can't we go back? Get under cover?"

"We're going back as far as the copter, but only because I have another heavy beamer stashed there. And then we're coming right back and we're going to locate that Tree—if I have to blast every damned plant between here and Tau Ceti."

The unhappy pair went stumbling away, and Selena sighed.

"I don't know what we're going to do, now. They won't be pleased at the state of their craft, but I can't see that stopping Pardoe now."

"The Tree's got him," Joe agreed grimly. "He'll be back."

It took just fifteen minutes to prove him right.

"Looks like we're stuck," Joe declared softly. "The only way to stop Pardoe now would be to kill him, and neither of us can do that."

"What is everything all about, please?" Pierre Lacoste broke his sleep-walking stupor to ask it in a voice that betrayed his Gallic origin. "I keep trying to believe it is all a nightmare, no? But it hurts like real."

"It's real." Selena shook her head in the gloom. "Don't either of you feel anything, a kind of uneasiness or anything like that?"

"I do," Robin volunteered. "Sounds crazy, but its like somebody singing, a Lorelei kind of thing, a long way off. And a sort of itch to go and see what it's all about. That what you mean?"

"Not singing," Pierre contradicted. "It is more like a beautiful woman who is saying 'Come to me, and I will make you happy.' It is like that, but I do not know how. It is insane. Is it?"

"It's a tree," Selena told them. "Believe it or not. Look, you've both heard stories, most of them fabulous, about Jensen's Planet and the miraculous Tree, haven't you? Well, this is it, and that's it, and it's all true—nearly all, anyway. This is no time to argue, or to explain. Just accept it. Buck Pardoe has, and he's on his way to the Tree right now, following the feeling that you have."

"You make that sound like the end of the world, Selena."

"It could be, Robin. We were hoping and trying to stop him, but short of shooting him down in cold blood from ambush, I don't see how we can, now. It would be absolute insanity to try to tackle him openly, the mood he's in and with the armory he has."

"I could kill him in cold blood, or hot blood, or any other kind," Pierre muttered. "But I am too much of a coward to try it."

"Don't run yourself into the ground," Delmar advised. "We never claimed to be professional heroes, did we? I still can't take it in—that noise in my mind is a tree? And that stuff about Jensen's Planet, is real? Even if so, what's so desperate about it?"

"This is no time to explain, Robin, even if I could without getting it all wrong. But you could try, for size, the idea of putting the ultimate weapon into the hands of a psychopath like Pardoe."

"Maybe you'll think better on a full stomach," Joe said, out of a long silence. "How long since you two ate?"

Selena felt instant contrition, deepened when both men revealed they had been given nothing at all; they had neither eaten nor had anything to drink since leaving their own ship.

"That's almost forty-eight hours. You must be starving! Joe, can we do anything about that?"

"No trouble at all. You ready?"

"Yes, but—what about Pardoe and the girl?"

"We can't do anything to them or about them, not now. The Tree wouldn't let us, now that it's curious about them. Come on."

Twenty minutes of traveling brought them to food and a cool stream where they could all refresh themselves and regain some measure of ease. But, with that out of the way, the main problem remained.

"They must surely have reached the Tree by now, Joe. Can you tell, from here?"

"By inference," he said. "I was following them, and then they just blended into the background. About five minutes ago. That means they are inside the main area of influence."

"So there isn't anything we can do at all, now?"

"We can follow, if you like, and see what happens. You want to try that? Bring your friends; I'll lead. Better keep a touch on me, Selena, just in case something goes wrong."

"I will," she promised, ridiculously pleased at his first use of her name. "You will be careful, Joe, won't you?"

He went away as silently and smoothly as ever, and even with her new senses, it was difficult to keep up, so she didn't try. It was all right as long as she could keep a mental touch on him. Despite her helpful guidance, her two companions made heavy weather of the dark jungle.

"You must have eyes like a cat," Robin complained, picking himself up from his third fall over sprawling roots.

"That is one thing. What else I do not understand is the plants," Pierre muttered. "Before, they were pulling and clutching with hooks and stings, as if they were alive. But not now."

She was ready to explain when the words died in her throat. Suddenly there was a sense of something missing, an emptiness. Robin and Pierre felt it, too. The Tree—it had stopped calling.

SEVENTEEN

THE ABSENCE of that pervading intelligence was almost a pain to her, like the death of a friend. Pierre put it in almost the same words.

"She has died—the so-beautiful woman who called me!"

"Something just switched off, that's for certain," Robin said. "What the hell, Selena?"

"I don't know." Confused notions came and went in her mind. Her intended explanation that the plants were sentient, that all one had to do was feel friendly—seemed vapid and unnecessary now. So, too, was her own tentative discovery, that the Tree presented itself in different ways to different people, or, possibly, that each individual interpreted the call in his own way. Whichever it was, it didn't matter. The Tree was dead—or was it? She led the way towards where Joe was waiting, a silent shadow just a few feet clear of the veil of leaves.

"What's happened?" she demanded anxiously, and he shrugged.

"No idea. This is new to me. I've never known the Tree to shut right off like this."

"Do you suppose Pardoe burned it, with his weapon?"

"I doubt it would keep still for anything like that. It can detect a threat just as fast as any of the other plants. Faster."

They stood awhile in silence; their common concern made it a companionable silence. She tried to think aloud.

"Pardoe got this far—got through. Got right up to the Tree and touched it. We can assume that."

"And the Martine female," he added grimly. "It sucked them both dry, because that's how it works. But then what?"

"We have to go in there and find out, Joe. I can't detect a thing beyond that curtain. Can you?"

"Not a smell. Friendly is all curled up in a ball. He doesn't like it one bit."

She shivered, put out her hand to take his, and felt his fingers grip on hers in sudden need.

"No way of telling what will happen if we go in there, Selena."

"Yes, I know. But we have to find out. And we have to believe that it won't hurt us."

"I'd like to believe that, too. All right, let me go ahead."

"No, not this time. You're handier than I am, Joe, just in case you have to take Pierre and Robin back—to my ship—where the Navy will be landing—in case—you know?" She let his hand go and went forward to the curtain. It was strangely still; not a leaf quivered. She reached out and pushed the fronds aside; they were stiff, almost waxy and stayed parted where she had pushed them, leaving a gap. She went into darkness in which she could perceive nothing at all. Could it be that the Tree had snatched back its gift in a moment of anger? That didn't seem likely, or even possible. She probed and got the feeling that it wasn't her ability that was at fault, but that something like a fog pervaded the whole grove. She had the creepy sense of trying to move into an occluded mind. There was a dull pain, a headache of immense proportions. She aimed her mind at the Tree itself.

"You're hurt," she told it. "You're upset in some way. I can tell that much, but I don't know any more than that. I want to help. Please let me help you. Tell me what I can do. Let me help!"

There was neither pretense nor effort in her call. She really did want to help. Something came to her from the Tree, for the murk around her seemed to swirl and eddy in quick agitation, ghostly fingers of breeze caressing her skin. Then, gradually, the darkness dwindled and vanished and the churchlike dimensions of the grove came into her ken. There was the massive, looming trunk of the Tree, and it ached to her touch. There were blotches on it. She looked around more by habit than from need, for she had already sensed the presence of the two others there. She turned and called.

"Joe! I think it's all right. I don't know what's happened, not yet, but I think it's all right."

He was beside her in a moment, his hand out to take hers in a way that struck warmth into her heart over the sorrow that filled the air.

"It's had a hell of a knock," he whispered. "Do you reckon we can do anything sensible to help?"

"Let's see what happened to those two first. I can't get anything from them. They're just lumps."

Together they paced across the turf to where the intruders were, and halted as a distinct shock tingled them both.

"What?" he grunted, whirling swiftly, and then he relaxed, and she eased also, as she saw. Pierre and Robin had followed, through the gap in the curtain, but only a few steps. Now they stood quite still, frozen like wax models in a store window.

"Poor thing," she murmured in instant understanding. "It can't stand any more strangers."

"I'm not surprised. But they won't come to any harm for a while. Let's look at Pardoe."

It was what she had come to do, but she regretted the necessity as soon as she was able to see just what was left of the crook. He was sprawled on the turf in a shapeless heap that could hardly be described as squatting, or crouching, or anything else. He was just a shapeless mass of flesh and bone, slumped and helpless, his head sagging down between his knees. Joe reached down, took a handful of hair and hoisted up that heavy head so that they could see his face.

"Nothing there," he muttered, and she had to compress her lips to keep her stomach down where it belonged, for Joe was literally correct. It was a slack and idiot-empty face, devoid of anything like wit or sanity. There was nothing at all. Just a helpless, brainless vegetable.

"Scraped him right out, and there was nothing to put back."

"Joe—that's horrible! And it's probably true, which makes it worse."

"No worse than a whole lot of people I've known." Joe was grimly calm.

Scorpia Martine was very beautiful but just as empty. "She's withdrawn—gone completely."

"They got what they wanted, in a way," he said, taking her in his arms. "I guess the Tree knows a lot more about humans now than it did before."

"But it's all wrong! It's got us all wrong. Somehow it has to learn that those two—"

"Strikes me it doesn't want to know any more about any of us, the way it cooled off your friends. Can you blame it, Selena? I mean, take a look at the trunk there, where those two touched it."

She turned her head to stare. There were angry splotches like scars on the dark smoothness. She eased herself free of his arms and went towards the trunk urgently.

"Don't do it," he called. "Don't—you don't know—"

"I have to. Someone has to show it—" She reached out for the massive trunk, took a breath, and there was Joe at her side.

"Takes two," he muttered. They reached out and touched as one. She felt instant twisting pains in her arms and shoulders, then all over—and caught her breath—but the twinges went as fast as they had come and replacing them came a vast curiosity, a wondering. She spoke aloud because it was the simplest way of arranging her thoughts to make sense.

"I'm sorry you've been hurt and upset. It couldn't be

helped. There *are* people like that. We don't like them any more than you do."

"That's right," Joe endorsed. "We don't like them. The only way anyone can tell what they are like is by finding out, by getting to know them; there's no other way. After a while you'll get to know them by—"

He stopped, and she knew why. Something had gone, dissolved, was no longer there. She looked at him in surmise, but he shrugged and dropped his hands.

"I don't know, Selena. I'm no psychologist, and I doubt if even a proper headshrinking expert would get very far with this. Fugue?"

"I was just about to say the same thing. Flight from reality —all three of them, in different degrees. Pardoe has lost his identity altogether. Miss Martine is inturned, catatonic. And now the Tree has withdrawn itself. Some time ago you said 'Ashamed of being human.' I think I would agree with that, now." She turned away from the lifeless trunk miserably, and distant movement caught her attention. Robin and Pierre came groping in what was, for them, dense gloom broken only by fitful starlight through interstices in the high vault of leaves.

"So this is the famous Tree?" Delmar put his head back to assess the size of it. "It's big, certainly."

"Impressive," Pierre agreed. "So far as one can see. But it is only a tree, after all."

Selena exhanged rueful glances with Joe. He looked sad, and she felt it, as if he had lost an old and valued friend. And yet, she had to be philosophical about it, the Tree had learned something valuable—how to shut itself off from harm and interference.

"Ah well," she sighed. "Perhaps we should be thankful that's all it is. The next problem is, somehow, to get these two back to my ship by the time the Navy gets here."

That took three of the roughest and most arduous days Selena had ever known. Pardoe—the empty shell of him— had to be fed, led, constantly prodded, urged, and watched. Miss Martine was easier, but still a worry, because she would just stop like a mechanical doll as soon as she was left alone. Robin and Pierre were willing but ignorant of the area. Selena came to marvel at Joe's infinite patience and resource, and discovered resources in herself that she had not dreamed she possessed. At the end of those three dreadful days her erstwhile playboy friends had acquired poise, alertness, and muscles. She had grown to feel as close to Joe as the fingers on one hand. It was a comradeship that owed little to words. Somehow she felt little need, or urge, to talk everything out as she had been so accustomed to do. Now it was a silent understanding, shared emotions, knowing what he was going to do next, finding him always ready and anticipating *her* next move; it was a warm thing.

She missed him within moments of sighting the bright spike of her ship. There was relief at their safe arrival, the blessed feeling of being able to relax, the outspoken pleasure of Robin and Pierre at the sight of something familiar and re-assuring—and then, in the middle of it all, he had vanished. She couldn't believe it at first. Then, when she tried pushing out her new senses as far as it was possible to stretch them, and finding no trace, she knew it was so, and that he had once again dropped out and gone into hiding. That was the evening of the third day. That night she slept once again in her own narrow bunk, bathed and clean, between silky sheets and with metal walls and watchdog circuits between her and the hazards of the wild outside—and she felt suf-focated and shut in.

The Navy arrived the following day, just before noon, with urgent messages crackling in her radio, and busy black dots high up in the blue, jockeying for orbit. It was an im-pressive force. Two medium-heavy cruisers, two shuttle ships, and one enormous research monitor, a space-borne laboratory complex crammed with specialists, their equipment, all hand-picked for just this moment. The range of disciplines cov-ered the whole spectrum of anything that could possibly apply to botanical biology, plus a more than fair complement of psychologists and psychiatrists, all unanimous in being firmly confident that there could be no such thing as sen-tient vegetation, but all equally determined to be there, just in case.

Admiral Longstaffe was in the first shuttle to touch ground. He had been briefed by radio about the immediate essentials—beware of the bushes—think friendly thoughts—and he was sensible enough to heed the advice. Selena greeted him warmly, very fit and honey-tanned, efficiently conventional in a fresh set of disposable coveralls, and was secretly amused to see the way his eyes widened at sight of her.

"No need to ask if you are well, my dear. One look is enough. And this is M. Lacoste, and Mr. Delmar? Congratulations, gentlemen. I'm told you were to a large degree instrumental in locating this planet. I'll want a word with both of you on that, later."

"And we need help with these two." Selena showed him the unfortunate victims of the Tree, and watched as trained personnel took charge.

"And now," Longstaffe declared, "what about the Tree?"

EIGHTEEN

"YES," she said soberly. "We found it. I can give you the coordinates. You have a walkabout there?" She meant the radio that linked Longstaffe with at least one other of his men at all times. As he nodded she resumed, "Better have all your department heads listen in, and make a recording, otherwise you'll all be asking the same questions several times over. And there's too much of it for that. In the first place, when I tell you just where the Tree is, and you mount an expedition, pick good men and women for it. I do not mean technically capable people. I mean good as in honest, sincere, clean-minded—with integrity. You'll see why when I explain the whole thing."

Longstaffe gave her a hard look, but respected her enough to do no more than issue instructions for all senior research personnel to listen. Then she told them precisely what they needed to know, and all she knew, about the Tree itself and the rest of the plant life, so far as she understood it. Impersonal and objective reportage was no new exercise for her, and she did it competently, omitting several items of a purely personal nature. Nevertheless, there was a lot to tell, and by the time she was finished the first impatient wave of scientists were standing looking at the Tree while listening to her. Their guarded comments came back to her via the etherwaves.

"A sense of serenity," one reported, "but no positive activity. You would say it resembles fugue?"

"That's my guess. You'll work out your own diagnosis. All I'm saying is that for centuries, possibly, it knew nothing but what it had learned from other trees, plants and growing things. Then it met honest humans, if I may so describe Scout Jensen—and myself. One can presume a whole new and exciting world being opened up to it. On the basis of your own results with its seeds, you will admit that to be a reasonable assumption. Then, as I have explained, it was so unfortunate as to encounter two rather bad humans, two people who were repulsive even to normal people. Ask Lacoste and Delmar how they were treated, what they have to say about those two. The result? You people are the experts, the psychologists. You'll have your own names for what happens to a mind that believes everything is sweetness and light and then has everything go bad all at once. What will you call it, insanity, overwhelming doubt, flight?"

"This is one for the books," one of the behaviorists snorted. "A neurotic tree."

"That's your problem," she declared. "But I have a suggestion, for what it's worth. If we assume this Tree is merely a reserve of potential, and talent, without what we would call personality—and that the effect, the impact of fully developed human personalities on it has been disastrous, it seems that the wisest thing to do is to study it as a specimen —that is, study its growth pattern, soil conditions, habitat and all that. And then forget *it*, but use that knowledge to develop the seeds properly. And then train *them*. Grow them into the ways you want them to be, as you would grow and educate an intelligent animal—or a baby."

She had had time to think that one through, and it was just as well, because they had many questions. What helped to still the remaining skepticism was the undeniable mobility of the plants. Before that day was over all the researchers were busy, slipping readily into teams, to search for and identify the peculiar molecules which might be responsible, to dissect and examine sections of the plants, to do air, soil and water analyses, cosmic-ray studies, crustal radioactivity tests—and a group of them hovered around the Tree itself, checking it in every way they could devise.

Longstaffe went back to his command cruiser with the

third shuttle, taking Robin Delmar and Pierre Lacoste with him. They were to be sent home just as soon as his men had put them through a total interrogation and had impressed on them the importance of saying nothing whatever about the things they had seen and heard in the past four days. When that shuttle came back down, disgorging more scientists and technicians, it also yielded a tall, gaunt, gray-haired man, with a perpetual dry smile and Selena's gray eyes. She was quietly delighted to see him.

"I hope I didn't give you a scare, Dad. I know you don't like me being in this kind of work, and I worry because you might be worried."

"Don't." He gripped her hand once, then got out the pipe that he was seldom seen without. "I never bothered to tell you, child, but it was my gentle hint that opened the way for you to be considered by the Corps in the first place."

"I suspected something of the kind. I mean, when they sorted me out and offered me the chance to take their tests, I knew someone had been singing my praises."

"And why not?" Conway Ash fired up and wreathed himself in aromatic smoke for a moment. "I know people; I can pick 'em. That's all there is to my job—not expertise, just knowing how to pick the right people for the right job."

"That I can understand." She relaxed in the sunshine by his side, and watched the busy men and gadgetry. She had always been comfortably close to her father in this way, able to relax and talk to him as man to man. "What I don't quite get is how you happened to know about the Philosophy Corps anyway. From the inside, I know that they are—deliberately vague, dispersed, hard to get in touch with, and almost legendary. That is really their strength, that they have no official propaganda, no known chief, or head-quarters, and very nearly no rules, either. Very few people even believe there is such a corps, in fact. Something like this planet, until we found it."

"Let you in on a secret." He smiled. "I was one of the founding members of the Corps. Had to pull out because I had talents that were more useful elsewhere. But I keep in touch; I can pull strings occasionally."

"I might have known! Tell me, what's going to happen to this planet, and the Tree?"

"Well now." He emitted a blue plume and studied it.

She knew that he was in fact watching her like a hawk. "I was going to ask you one—why are you hanging on here? Nothing more you can do. Your friends have gone. You're not technical enough to contribute anything further. What's the attraction?"

"It's a lovely place," she said promptly and demurely, and he snorted gently. "I'd like to live here," she added, and he snorted again.

"Bad luck. I've been through the preliminary assessments. We are going to invoke Secregs on this one, make it Q-max."

"Quarantine?" She frowned over that for a moment, then nodded. "Yes, I suppose that's sensible. It's hardly ideal for open colonization as it stands, and it wouldn't be wise to leave it unguarded for more enterprising people like Pardoe and company. But total quarantine? Wouldn't you want to leave someone here, in charge? A look-out?"

"Look out for what? There'll be a network of watch-dog satellites and alarms. And eventually, maybe, we will put down a base team, but not for a long while yet—some years. The scientists will gather and take away enough material to keep them busy that long. You see, if we can't grow the plants and make them do tricks in our laboratories, or in some spot of our own choosing, there's not a lot of point, is there? So who needs a ground base? And, in any case," he added, so negligently that she fell right into it, "who would want to stay here in this wilderness?"

"I would," she said grinning as he stirred just a little. "You like sneaking up on people, don't you? All right, now you know. I want to stay here."

"You look well on it. That glow isn't just health; Selly, I know you that well. There's only one thing could make you offensively radiant like that and willing to pull out of the Corps at the same time. Want to tell me about him?"

She was relieved to be able to talk, and Conway Ash was a good listener. "It wasn't," she admitted, "until I was slanging him for being a drop-out—tucking himself away in the Scout Service, and then here—that I realized I was talking about myself, too. I don't belong anywhere. All my life I've been pretending to be this, that and the other. The only reason I liked being in the Corps was because it set me apart from the herd. And above them, too—and that's not good. I don't belong out there. But I am at home here."

"All right. It's your life. He sounds quite a character. The way you've drawn him, I don't blame him for hiding out. But, supposing you do find him, and he doesn't think the way you do, then what happens?"

"It's a big planet. I really do like it here, Dad. Leave me a caller, and I'll be official guide and advisor to the base team, when you do send one. But not for a year, please?"

"All right again. May I offer just one piece of advice? That research monitor up there is stuffed with psychologists of all kinds. You have a chat with some of them, learn up a bit. It can't hurt, and in my opinion that boy of yours needs help. You do that, eh?"

"You're ahead of me, as always. I was intending to do just that."

She had her chances. It took the researchers almost four weeks of concentrated effort to get all the material they needed, and for the Navy to establish a four-unit network of guardian satellites, small and far out, almost invisible, but triggered to give warning should anyone try to orbit and land on the planet. Eventually, though, the shuttles went off into the blue for the last time. Temporary base cabins were dismantled and shipped out; people went away in groups—one small crew took care of her own ship and lifted it to swing with the rest—and the planet was still and silent once more.

She was prepared for a long wait. She had managed to find Joe's old ship; it had not been easy because he had allowed the landing feet to settle deep into the soft earth and had encouraged creepers and flowering shrubs of all kinds to drape themselves around it until it was like a part of the living forest, but she found it. Without her special sense of space she might never have succeeded. Having located it, she took no liberties, but made herself at home in a discreet manner with the minimum of disturbance, like a guest. He had made sure it would never fly again, but it was otherwise quite functional and comfortable. There were book tapes and musicassettes enough to make sure she would not be bored, even if she had not had ploys of her own to occupy the time.

Part of her task was to get to know the friendly flowers

all about his home and to revive his custom of playing them tunefull and rhythmic music. They really did prefer waltzes, and it was great fun for her to sit and be aware of their pleasure in the music. Another thing she did was to discard all the artificial trappings of civilization. *"Consider the lilies of the field . . ."* She had quoted the lines from Matthew often, but never until now had she realized the point of them. Quite happily, she went naked and was at one with the peaceful and unspoiled world about her. Warmed in the sun by day, securely dreamless and untroubled by night, she settled into a serene and quiet bliss she had never before believed possible, a state of mind that took her back to the carefree, semi-mystical days of her childhood. And, like a child, she had mischief in mind.

It was in the early afternoon of the ninth day that he came back. She was aware of his approach long before he came into sight, and she assumed that he was likewise aware of her presence. She had counted on it and prepared against it as part of her mischief. She sat, quite still and at ease, on the warm turf by the ship's gangway foot, and waited, sensing his slow movement, guessing at his suspicions and waiting for him to appear through a break in the bushes across the glade from where she was. The slanting sun was on his face as he stood there, gripping his spear and swinging his head from side to side in bewilderment.

"Selena?" he said very softly and in doubt. She kept silent, stealing this precious moment to study him and refresh her memory. He looked lost and baffled searching for her, although she was in plain view.

"It's a trick," he said. "You're playing a trick on me. Where are you?"

"I'm here, Joe. It's all right." She rose and went to him, took his arm and led him back to where she had been sitting. "Yes, I played a trick on you. Several tricks, in fact, but none of them malicious—"

"I watched the ships go. I thought everyone had gone. I thought they would quarantine the planet."

"They did. It's a Q-Max. There'll be no one coming back here for at least a year, and then only a research team. You're quite safe now."

"But you're here. You stayed."

"Do you mind that very much?"

"I don't understand." He looked lost and troubled. "Why are there so many of you—like echoes?"

"I made friends with your friendly plants, Joe, and I trained some of them, four of them, to play a trick on you—on your Friendly. He is picking me up all over the place, isn't he? And, all the time, I am here, right by your side." She touched his hand again, and he shook his head.

"You know?"

"I've known for a long time, Joe, that you're blind."

NINETEEN

HE SAT, just where he was, and she settled down beside him, to reach and take his hand again. It was quite still in hers.

"How long have you known?"

"Almost from the beginning, Joe. You have a very direct stare, and I learned long ago that only abnormal people stare steadily like that. Either they do it on purpose—or the person isn't really looking at all. And then, those binoculars. You hadn't used them in so long, you not only forgot where you'd put them, you also forgot to slip back the lens covers. Yet you pretended to look through them, for my benefit. And you never did mention the color of anything, even the red blossom I put in my hair; you let me call it blue. So I knew, but it wasn't until the Tree gave me the power to sense masses and shapes—like Friendly—that I realized how wonderfully you could manage. So I don't feel sorry for you. If you're all ready to recoil from pity, don't be."

"Why did you stay behind?"

"To any other man the reason would be obvious. If it was any other woman but me, that would be the right reason, too. It might well be"—she hesitated at it—"one of the reasons. There are others. One is that I like this place; I really do. There's another, not so simple. To explain it, I want you to sit still and listen while I tell you a story, a story about a man called Jory Jensen, a Navy Scout."

"He's dead."

"Yes, yes, he's dead. In a way, he is. I know a lot about Jory Jensen. Before I ever came to this planet I had studied his dossier, the full record in the Navy files, so I know all that. But I know a lot more than that, too. I know how and where he died. He was a strange man, an eccentric one, but a good man. To be a scout a man needs to be a bit of an oddball, but Jensen was a near-genius. He could have been away up at the top in anything he tried—but he couldn't stand people—stupid, non-rational, whimsical, emotional, immature people. He was *too* good. It is nothing unusual, that. Such people go strange trying to fit in, or they opt out. Jensen opted out, as a scout. And he was a good one.

"And then one day he happened on a planet of a system that was different. He went through all the routine steps, but he kept running into the awareness that this place was different: pleasant, clean, good, and welcoming. He felt at home. So he omitted to include it in his flight log. And he kept on coming back to this place between commissions. He would have staked a personal claim, but a scout is not allowed to do that, so he had to go on hoping that no one else would ever land on it. And it preyed on his mind. He worried. He had found a wise old tree on this planet and made friends with it. On one trip he had a small accident, nothing serious, and the Tree cured him—just like that. That's when he began to realize what he had found. And then—the law of averages caught up with him. He had a bad accident with his drive, and got an overdose of mu-radiation. He didn't know for sure, but he suspected. He patched up the job and came on home—"

"How do you know all that?" he queried, and she squeezed his hand.

"Part of the job. The mechanics went over his ship for a fast preliminary, spotted the repair, made it good, and reported it while they made an estimate as to the rest of the overhaul. Meanwhile, Jensen went in for his routine checkup, and they gave him a blue card. That was enough to confirm what he suspected. He ran, got back to his ship before anyone thought to slap a distraint on it, and blew. According to the official book he headed out into the big dark and died."

"That's mu-radiation," Joe muttered. "There's no cure."

"Just so. That's fact. The rest is guesswork, but with some

supporting grounds. Jory Jensen came to this planet. He knew what the Tree could do, he hoped it could cope with mu-radiation. He tried—and it did. It was a big job, and in the process Jory got changed quite a bit. A complete overhaul, you might say. You might also say that he was not the same man he had been. So, you might say, Jory Jensen is dead. But you're alive, Joe."

"And blind!"

"Yes. I've been thinking about that. You say the Tree can't understand sight, because it's just a tree. And that's true enough. But there's another side to that, Joe. Those ships that came, and went away again, were stuffed to the rivets with psychologists of all kinds. That's obvious, isn't it? I mean—intelligent plants? So, I've always been interested in psychology and its application to sociology, too. I talked with them. About you. Not by name," she added quickly, as his fingers twitched. "More in the nature of a hypothetical question. And the answers were illuminating. To start with, the effect of mu-radiaion is to induce a slow but irreversible decay in the nervous system. It goes, bit by bit. The senses are the first to shut down. No need to go into all of it, but let's get this straight. You're cured completely. You wouldn't be here otherwise. Is that understood?"

"Not by me, it isn't. I'm still blind!"

"And feeling a bit sorry for yourself?"

He lifted up and away from her all in one sinuous movement, and his face was bleak, like weathered timber. "I'm happy here. I have Friendly. I get by. This is my home."

"I touched a nerve, didn't I, Joe?—admit it. Come back here and face it—and listen." She waited, steeling her heart to be hard and as ruthless as was necessary. He came and sat, defiantly. She reached for his hand again. "Here's a question for you, Joe. Suppose you could see again? Just suppose it could be fixed? Would it make any difference?"

"None at all. I like it here. I'm all through and washed up with people. I decided that when I knew I was losing my sight. What good is a blind scout? I dropped out, as you say. But then, I learned to live with it, with Friendly to help. And this is my home, now, sight or not." He hesitated at that, and she could feel his mind working along with his uneasy fingers. After a while he added, "I don't mind you being here. I thought you had gone along with the rest, and

I was a bit sorry about that. I had begun to think that you could fit in here."

"Thank you. I'm glad; I like it here. I was thinking that I fitted in, too, but I was quite ready to move away to some other spot. I don't want to be in your way."

"That's all right; you belong. But let's not have any more of that about me feeling sorry for myself."

"Why not? Wouldn't you like to be able to see again?"

"I can see all I want to, with Friendly."

"Just so. And that tells me quite a bit. Here's part of it. You say a tree can't see, knows nothing of sight. That's true. Sight is more than just a functional optical system, though. Eyes don't see, Joe. *You* see, with and through your eyes; and your eyes are perfectly all right, Joe. There's nothing wrong with them."

This time he didn't jerk up and away. He sat quite still, but his fingers were tense in hers. "That's not a very good joke," he said quietly. "It's not funny. Do you think I'm just pretending to be blind?"

"No, not quite that. I want you to do something for me, please. It won't take long. And I promise, afterwards, I will go away and leave you alone, if that's what you want. Please?"

"More tricks?"

"In a way, but I'm trying to help not to hurt. You *do* know me better than that, surely?"

"All right, what do I do?"

"Stand up. Stand up just there. Right—now take off your friendly plant, right off and away." As he hesitated she added, "It's quite all right, I'll take care of him, and you shall have him back. I promise."

Highly unwillingly he peeled out of his fiber harness, carefully easing away the coils of the plant-stem from his chest and shoulder.

"I'm all in the dark now," he muttered. She took the small warm bundle and laid it aside, and smiled at him.

"All in the dark and helpless—I know. You fear that, and quite naturally. But not just now. You're with friends, Joe, including me. Just think about that for a moment."

"All right," he muttered. "There's no danger. So?"

"So," she said, mocking him gently, "now shut your eyes. Go on, it can't make any difference, can it?" He shrugged, closed his eyes, and she stood back a few paces from him, facing him, put an edge on her voice.

"Think, Joe, think hard. Think, Jory Jensen that was, and tell me true. What is it that you don't want to see? What is it you're afraid to face? What are you hiding from? Is it guilt? Do you feel guilty because you've dropped out—dodged your responsibilities? Abandoned your career, your duty, your Service oath? What? What is it that you are refusing to see?" She threw the words at him like darts, leaning on them, putting them in deep as she had been taught, striking right down to his hidden values, stirring up the submerged fears.

She saw him shake and dwindle like a stricken tree. He choked on words that were difficult to get out. Then, in a burst, they came.

"Humanity! You can keep it, have it, forget it—lying, cheating, grubbing, stinking—the whole filthy mess—you can have it all. I want no part of it!"

"You're so right," she agreed. "That's the way humanity is, part of the time. And you are part of it; you're a human being, too."

"No! The hell with it. I want no part of it. I'm out."

"It's no good, Joe. Shutting your eyes to it won't make it go away. It's still here. You think you've gone away from it, but you can't get away from yourself. You can't! Face it, Joe; look at it. Look at me, Joe. I'm human, too. Look at me —you can. You *know* you can. You're not afraid of me, surely? Look at me, Joe. Come on now, look!"

Then she caught her breath, just watching him sweat and struggle, and then open his eyes. And her heart turned over—because he *could* see. It was obvious. The expression on his face was enough to prove it. She stood quite still, blinking at ridiculous tears and trying to smile—and then she held out her arms to him. But he shook his head as if dazed, and the light in his eyes was something to behold.

"No magic," she whispered, suddenly embarrassed. "Don't think that—just applied psychology. Psychic blindness is nothing new nor strange. It's common enough. Joe, don't—"

"Selena!" he said, and there was that in his voice that made heat in her cheeks and giddiness in her heart. "You're beautiful. So beautiful! Friendly told me you were lovely, but I never dreamed—I can see you—and you're much more beautiful than I ever dreamed."

"It was a chance I had to take," she mumbled, suddenly and dizzily aware that she was completely nude. "I'm so glad it worked—and that you think I'm—nice to look at!"

"I would have known you by your voice. But you—you're so beautiful, I could go on looking at you—I can see!" A shadow darkened his delight. "I can see; you cured me. Now I'll have to go back."

"Oh no you won't," she said, suddenly in charge again, and very positive. "No one knows anything about you except me—and Dad. I had to tell him, you see, because I've dropped out, too. I'm official resident here, at least for a year. And, if I like it at the end of that time, it will be permanent. I think I am going to like it here, but that's really up to you, isn't it? Now that you can see, you may not think that I belong—"

"You belong more than ever, Selena. I'd sooner be blind again than lose you now. I can ask you honestly now, please stay."

"I was hoping you'd ask. You see, my dear, my motives for wanting you to be able to see were not quite impersonal. They were rather selfish, really. Tell me again, am I really so beautiful?"

AFTERWORD

SAFELY BACK in his office on Luna, Admiral Longstaffe took out and re-read the personal memo that Selena had handed him just before he left the planet.

TO Longstaffe, Adml., SEC/CHEF U.P. Off. TECH/ STRAT.
FROM Selena Ash, P.C.
RE Jensen's Planet.

Please have the enclosed standard one-square-mile territorial claim processed for me soonest. I haven't yet chosen my spot, but I promise it will be nowhere near the Tree.

When you report to P.C. H.Q. on my behalf, please inform them I hope to be able to recruit a new boy, if I can open his eyes for him.

Finally, when you mark off the date on your calendar one year from now, please include in the party one multi-denominational padre. One way or another, I mean to get this one. Wish me luck.

"Luck?" Longstaffe sighed as he filed the papers carefully and made the necessary calendar notation. "That's like taking an ore crusher to crack an egg. By God, if I was thirty years younger you wouldn't have to twist *my* arm!" And he sighed again. *Some folk,* he thought, *have all the luck.*

ACE BOOKS

SCIENCE-FANTASY ANTHOLOGIES

The best authors and their best stories are sure to be in these top-rated collections of science fiction and fantasy.

WORLD'S BEST SCIENCE FICTION: 1969   91352 — 95¢
Edited by Donald A. Wollheim & Terry Carr

WORLD'S BEST SCIENCE FICTION: 1968   91351 — 75¢
Edited by Donald A. Wollheim & Terry Carr

THE "IF" READER OF SCIENCE FICTION   36330 — 60¢
Edited by Frederik Pohl

NEW WORLDS OF FANTASY   57270 — 75¢
Edited by Terry Carr

**THE BEST FROM FANTASY AND SCIENCE
FICTION: THIRTEENTH SERIES**   05452 — 60¢
Edited by Avram Davidson

**THE BEST FROM FANTASY AND SCIENCE
FICTION: FOURTEENTH SERIES**   05453 — 75¢
Edited by Avram Davidson

**THE BEST FROM FANTASY AND SCIENCE
FICTION: FIFTEENTH SERIES**   05454 — 75¢
Edited by Edward L. Ferman

Available from Ace Books (Dept. MM), 1120 Avenue of the Americas, New York, N.Y. 10036. Send price indicated, plus 10¢ handling fee.

ACE RECOMMENDS . . .